To the Sm
Debt

QUEENS
CRESCENT

BY

JEREMY
GOODCHILD,

I hope you enjoy it!
Thank you for all the
Lovley Lockdown Songs.
& your wonderful Humour!
all my.
love Y

Jeremy G.
xxx.

1

For my friends and readers,
may this give you a good laugh wherever
you are.

This is a work of fiction. Names, characters, places and incidents either are products of the author's imagination or are used fictitiously. Any resemblance to actual events or locales or persons, (unless specifically named) living or dead, is entirely coincidental. This book is not for the faint hearted or woke types who live by politically correct ideology. If you are easily offended, or dislike bad language and vulgarity, I suggest you put this book down now. You have been warned!

Queens Crescent is a small cul-de-sac of detached houses on the outskirts of Brighton in East Sussex England.

Built in the year 2015. Stylish but reasonably affordable homes, they attracted a fair amount of interest, having easy access by bus into the centre of Brighton. Three and 4 bedroom houses with decent size plots and gardens. Those in the know got their names down quickly as soon as the plots went up for sale and the show home was opened. Decent new housing in the Brighton area being rare. Having been tipped off by a local gay councillor, local drag Legend Daisy Froglette was able to put the word about quickly when performing his cabaret act at the popular gay entertainment venue The Fawcett Inn.

Consequently, those in the front of the queue happened to be gay couples, delighted by the show home and the plans. Cheque books were whipped out and £1000 deposits put down almost immediately.

The delighted builders soon got the new estate up and running and by the summer of 2016 all the residents had moved into their brand new homes.

Let me introduce you to the neighbours

live Frank 55 and Josh 40. Frank and Josh are the landlords of The Fawcett Inn off of St James Street in Brighton. Frank an ex Sergeant Major in the army and Josh a chef and cabaret singer/male model, are both actual real Brightonian's. Unusual in such a transient city as Brighton.

Frank is 6 foot and physically fit, shaved head, piercing blue eyes and a cropped beard now grey. Josh a good looking 5 feet 10 Italian looking god. They are an extremely popular couple on ~Brighton's gay scene and The Fawcett Inn is packed out most nights. They bought No 1 as a bolt hole so they could get away from the business occasionally and to own a normal home. They had met in Sitges in Spain 15 years ago and are a happy couple with two Dogs.

No 2 Queens Crescent

---

live Roz 42 and Yolanda.42

The girls had met on a cycling holiday in Wales in 2005. Roz a chubby butch type, short and stocky with cropped dark hair and tattoos, works as a bouncer on the door of a club in Brighton Marina. She fell in love at first sight with Yolanda an Infant school teacher in charge of art and drama. A pretty slim woman, with long curly brown hair and a figure to die for. They hit it off immediately, although they have little in common. Yolanda is very political and goes on any peace rally or climate change demo going, she's a strict vegan, ardent feminist and remainer and a big campaigner for transgender rights. She votes Green or Labour (A Corbynista) depending how much in love with Caroline Lucas she is at the time.

Roz on the other hand leans more to the right politically, is instinctively anti EU tends to vote Tory and loves nothing more than a 12 oz rare rib eye steak with triple fried chips or a huge Gutbuster breakfast at the all night diner after she's downed 12 pints of Kronenburg on her night off.

However, Roz love's Yo and doesn't let on and pretends to go along with what Yo says for an easy life. Yolanda is also a friend of the gay councillor in the planning department of Brighton and Hove council, they go on marches together and share a yoga guru.

No 3 Queens Crescent

Lives John 38 and Grant 34

John a builder 5"10 muscular bear type, a cheeky chappy with blue eyes and a wicked laugh shaved head and hairy chest, met Grant when Grant hired John to build a garden extension on his mother's house in Saltdean.

John was originally from Battersea in London had been married to a woman and had two children a boy and a girl, James and Katy. He had left his wife Sarah after "coming out" and moved to Brighton after an angry and difficult divorce.

He met Grant 5 years before while he was very bruised, full of guilt and mentally messed up.

Grant tall 6" blonde blue eyed, tanned and muscular with a smooth honed body was a head turner. He had always looked after himself and had a "Hollywood smile"

They went out for a pint a few times after saying

hello at the gym. They both fell for each other straight away, but it took a long time for John to commit, because of his kids, but eventually they worked it out. Grant had a good head for business and he set up a new building contractors firm that specialised in home conversions and the two of them were permanently busy converting period homes in Brighton for the Islingtonista's that were moving down from London who all wanted eco-friendly, ethically sourced, open plan living spaces that cost a fortune. They bought a new home because they didn't want a doer upper themselves.

No 4 Queens Crescent

---

lives Michael 72, and Cecil 69

Originally from Oldham in Lancashire, they have been a couple for 40 years, 10 of them in secret. Michael was married with a family and Cecil lived around the corner with his mother. They lived in identical terraced houses a few yards from each other.

Michael (Mike) had been a miner then turned painter and decorator, after Margaret Thatcher closed his pit down. (something he secretly thanked god for) A huge stocky man 5"8 strong as an ox and heavily tattooed. Cecil owned a Hairdressers in the high street called Bona Riah. He is very tall 6"1 and very slim, naturally camp, he tried to suppress any sign of effeminacy at an early age due to bullies at school, without too much success. The ladies of Oldham said "he was not the marrying kind"

They had met in a cottage (public lavatory) in a park in Oldham. A notorious cruising area, they met here once a week for ages until they took the plunge and had a weekend together in Blackpool.

Agreeing to never speak to each other in the street if they ever saw each other they carried on this clandestine affair for 10 years, until Michaels children had left home, and his wife threw him out as she "wanted a real man to fuck"

She did them both a favour. Cecil sold the hairdressers and after a "honeymoon" in Benidorm (mother went too) they bought a boarding house in Blackpool with a basement flat for Cecil's mum Ruby. They ran this very successfully for years until Ruby died and Cecil heartbroken couldn't bear to stay in the hotel any longer. So, they upped sticks and moved to Brighton. There they rented a little flat in Kemp town until they decided where to buy. They were in The Fawcett Inn the night Daisy Froglette let slip about the new houses going up in Queens Crescent.

No 5 Queens Crescent

live Ben 42 and Gordon 38

Ben is a human rights lawyer, black, Oxford educated and deeply liberal politically, he commutes to work in London, A studious type, tall, bald and neat, physically fit due to working out every day in their home gym. He met Gordon, when Gordon a local estate agent showed him around his first flat in

Brighton. Gordon's ears pricked up when Ben said he was looking for a flat with strong ceilings and good sound proofing. Gordon a keen fan of S&M looked at Ben straight in the eye said would you like to see my place?

Gordon has a shaved head and a hipster beard, tall and thin, hairless on top but dark and hirsute underneath lived in a basement flat in Hove in a large Victorian house converted into flats. Gordon had spent a fortune converting the main bedroom into a dungeon. He had sound proofed it and reinforced the ceilings and walls. Every toy imaginable was on a large shelf next to a hoist with a leather sling with various straps. Hooked on the walls were handcuffs whips and various other items of restraint. Ben's eyes lit up with pleasure on viewing. He didn't need to be asked twice to move in after their initial session. Gordon had been on the lookout for a master like Ben with big hands and a big dick for a long time. Eventually though Ben got fed up with the lack of space in the dungeon flat and wanted to move to a house full of light where he could build his own home gym. They were just ordering their drinks when they heard Daisy Froglette mention Queens Crescent. Gordon being an astute estate agent got straight on the phone.

No 6 Queens Crescent

---

live Alistair 75 and Renaldo 38

Alistair a retired headmaster and old school gentleman, a slightly frail man who keeps his own council but is pleasant and polite, he always says good morning to his neighbours. A book worm and lover of old black and white films, He is handsome still in a distinguished kind of way. Grey hair, Van Dyke beard and a glint in his green eyes. He spends his days reading or watching Talking Pictures, his favourite TV channel, before preparing a gourmet meal for his adored younger partner Renaldo, a Spanish teacher at Brighton University.

They had met 12 years ago at a teacher training seminar where Alistair was giving a lecture. Renaldo was an exchange student from Valencia, he fell in love with Alistair and never went back, except for holidays. Renaldo was typically Spanish, very gregarious, warm and funny. Handsome dark looks but only 5"8 tall he loves to dance and sing and eat. He has gained a bit of a belly from eating Alistair's carefully prepared evening meals. He loves roast potatoes as much as tapas. He has taken up yoga to try and lose some weight, where he became friendly with Yolanda and the councillor. He had never liked living in a bungalow in Peacehaven and persuaded Alistair to move to Queens Crescent.

No 7 Queens Crescent

Live Karl 67 and Kris 66

These two met performing in 42nd Street in the 1980's. After a hugely successful west end run, they signed up to go on the touring version as well. It is their life. Kris (Kristabelle) was in the chorus as was Karl who was also a talented dressmaker and costume designer.

Both tall at 6 feet, their whole life is about "showbiz" Not a natural match as a couple you might think but something works between them. They are what was referred to years ago as Tootsie trade (both the same type) which would now be referred to in their case as "bottoms" But somehow, they make their "open" relationship work. Their mutual love of the theatre plus their acid sense of humour being a huge bond between them.

Kris had been a tall dark stunner when he was younger who looked a lot like George Michael, sadly those looks have faded now, basically down to an eating disorder and a love of gin and cigarettes. However, in the right dress and good make up and lighting they both could still look stunning when they appeared on stage at The Fawcett Inn and other drag pubs on the gay circuit, up and down the country as

"The Royal Sisters"

Karl (Karla) had also been a bit of a looker in his youth, blonde blue eyed. His only bad feature were slightly protruding teeth, but he used this to his advantage in some of the comedy numbers they performed in the act. Both were old friends of Daisy Froglette even if Daisy did refer to Kristabelle as Kristallnacht in her act. They were waiting to go on in the wings at The Fawcett Inn when they heard Daisy mention Queens Crescent.

No 8 Queens Crescent

Ollie 25 and Will 24 "The kids"

The youngest couple in Queens Crescent. They are referred to by all the neighbours as the kids and loved by them all.

Young good looking and successful they are a great team. Ollie is something very clever in IT and works from home. He is 5"11 dark haired with an Essex boy style quiff, designer stubble, a six pack and puppy dog eyes.

Will is 6"2 blonde blue eyes short cropped hair and very fit. He should be he's a personal gym coach at the Davina Lloyd Gym down at the marina. He also offers a full body massage from home or home visits. A popular service especially the full body service with a happy ending. So popular they have had to convert the garage into a massage therapy centre and are now offering 4 hand body massage with happy ending If required, Ollie being quite versatile, also works a couple of shifts a week at the Fawcett Inn and was just handing Ben and Gordon their change when he heard Daisy Froglette mention Queens Crescent.

Once a year the residents committee of Queens Crescent got together to arrange a summer fete for all the occupants of Queens Crescent and their friends and families and threw a huge party on the green opposite the houses. Being a private estate Queens Green was communal land owned by each of the owners. The estate agents Gordon from number 5 worked for called Mission Accomplished were the managing agents and collected the annual community fees for the upkeep of the green and flower beds. They had turned it into a pretty little park, with tasteful flower tubs and shrubs, some nice benches to sit on and a decked area with a large summer house at the end which doubled up as a tearoom and bar. They all mucked in and offered what skills they had and had turned it into a remarkably successful community project.

This year's theme was to be "Hollywood's Golden Era" Karl and Kristabelles idea which was met with more enthusiasm from the residents than Yolanda's had been last year. Each year each house could pick a theme, Yolanda's had been "wellbeing, mindfulness and fire eating" Kristabelle had commented the two things hardly go together dear do they! One slip and your whole hoop could go up like a Roman candle luv.

But it went ahead. Roz was up early each morning for 2 weeks erecting tents and tepees on loan from Brighton council, hammering in steaks into the ground with gusto. John and Grant mucked in with her at the weekends as did the kids. It soon looked like a mini pride. They had a Tarot reading tent. Yoga of course, A safe area where you could just go and sit on your own and sulk, holistic massage and a food tent which served vegan fayre of all varieties. Roz had even persuaded local MP Marion Mukas to come along (for a small fee) to cut the ribbon to open the Fete.

The entertainment had been a hippy band called the Magic Mushrooms so there was lots of drums and chanting and of course the fire eating. Most of the gang were dreading it. Some of their friends hadn't stayed long. Those that stayed joined in and after a few hours at the bar, courtesy of the Fawcett Inn, were to pissed to care. Even Ben and Gordon were dancing around the maypole and banging tambourines. Ben's mother had been a devout Salvation Army soldier when he was a boy in Brixton and he knew how to bang out a good rhythm, despite his large hands.

Plus, the kids had scored some really strong weed off of one of the Magic Mushrooms and were rolling joints for all and had sprinkled a fair bit in the aubergine and chickpea curry which everyone said was delicious. So, all in all a good do and everyone was REALLY happy.

But this year Karl and Kris were determined that the atmosphere would be different. There was a heated but enthusiastic discussion going on at number 7. Most nights when the gin bottle came out, the planning and details were being worked out, then discarded then revamped again. When alone and relaxed they dropped their usual haughty, grand, demeanour and reverted to their original south London dialect.

Karl was just refreshing the pint-sized crystal goblets with more ice and lemon and copious amounts of gin with a whisper of tonic said.

Well dear I know I've said it before but as it's our turn this year I want it to be ultra-glamorous, star spangled just like a night at the Oscars, Well, how the Oscars used to be when we had real stars like Judy Garland and Bette Davis. Not like now days with all these scruffy gits, rambling on about bleeding climate change and me too and all that bollocks.

Yes, what do they mean me too? said Kris, I've always said me too, I've never said no to fuck all dear. No that's your problem love you never could Karl said with a smirk.

Saucy cow said Kris you've hardly been the virgin Mary either dear. You've had more cocks up you then a Bernard Mathews battery hen.

Oh, dear the old ones are still the best said Karl dripping sarcasm. Can we get back to the party? I want a summer ball with proper entertainment and seating and a stage and lighting and a band. Yes, well I agree with you there dear said Kris, we don't want a repeat of last year do we. None of that sitting in a circle in a tent talking to our minges for hours dear. I could hardly walk when I got up, plus me arse was wet, I had terrible piles after. Oh, do give over Kris, how about this year what are we going to wear?

Meanwhile back at No 5 Gordon and Ben were up on a ladder in their new dungeon. One of the ceiling bolts had come loose the other night while Gordon was in the sling causing him to fall and tip sideways, luckily, he was strapped in or he could have gone headfirst. Ben instinctively reached out to grab him but slid off due to the amount of Crisco lube he had applied to his extremely large hands. Instead of steadying Gordon he knocked him further sideways, causing Gordon to impale himself on one of his favourite black dildos called the knobbly bobbly that was suction stuck on to the wall. Whilst enjoying the sensation he hadn't quite mentally prepared for the intrusion and yelled out loud in a high pitched tone. Ben suddenly saw the funny side of it and started laughing hysterically, which was unusual because being a deeply woke human rights activist he didn't really see the funny side to anything.

What are you laughing at you bastard? yelled Gordon while clinging on to a wrist cuff that was screwed to the wall. Get me down! Eventually released from the sling they both decided to call it a day and Ben settled for a wank.

Praying they had made adequate repairs to the ceiling bolt Gordon was looking forward to swinging back to happiness tonight. Ben had been on Grindr and invited a couple of heavy-set muscle Mary types over to share the workload.

John put his key in the door of number 3 and he and Grant wearily let themselves in. Grant went straight to the fridge and cracked open a couple of cold beers. They were both knackered. They had been working hard for weeks now on a massive conversion job on a house in Salisbury Road in Hove. Today they had managed to get 2 of the 8 solar panels fitted onto the roof of this lovely old Victorian mansion. One of the few houses left in the area that hadn't been converted into flats. A gay Labour MP called Paul Bryan had bought it a few months ago. He intended to live in it at weekends while renting out his London flat for a small fortune. He then rented another pied a tere near Westminster which he was able to claim the rent back from the taxpayer for living expenses. His constituency was up north somewhere which he only visited if he absolutely had to. Still he was a bit of a hard nut, he had been ridiculed by the press for posing nearly nude on Grindr in a pair of women's panties. He had just laughed it off. So what? I won't be the first MP to be caught like that. At least I didn't have an orange stuck in my mouth like that Tory who got caught out.

John finished his beer grabbed Grants hand and led him up to the bedroom. They both stripped off and went in their luxury wet room. Grant turned on all the taps and they stood there and let jets of hot water hit their hard worked bodies. They took it in turns to soap each other all over before rinsing off. Once dry they laid down on the bed and made love tenderly. John was very good with his tongue technique and drove Grant crazy as he explored every part of his body with his mouth and tongue. Once they had both satisfied each other they pulled on their comfy track bottoms and tee shirts and went downstairs. Cuddled up on the couch with a nice glass of chilled Chenin Blanc they ordered a Chinese takeaway while they watched 'Breaking Bad' on Netflix. Their idea of a perfect Friday night.

Have you seen my bag with the clipboards and my dabbers in Mike? Said Cecil Yes, it's under the stairs said Mike. Now get a move on Cecil at this rate we'll miss bus and be late for first T'house. Mike had a thick Lancashire accent, Cecil slightly less.

Okay I'm coming said Cecil thumping down the stairs in a new full length anorak, with a fur collar. What the Fook 'ave you got on there then? Said Mike. It's me new coat I ordered it from Matalan online it was reduced by 20 quid, said Cecil.

They saw you fooking coming, now come on you dozy cont get a move on.

Yer alright I'll just grab me bingo bag.

Friday night at number 4 meant one thing and one thing only, Bingo night. Every week the boys made their way down to the Buzz Bingo in Freshfield Road in Kemptown. They loved it. They met a lot of friends there. They sat with an old couple called Bob and Rita at the same table each week, but they knew lots of others there too. Bingo was surprisingly popular with the gay community in Brighton. It was

17

not unusual to see a couple of queens in full leather queuing for their books or at the bar. Much waving and kiss blowing went on before the caller started the first session. As bingo finished fairly early those who went could head straight out for the bars in St James Street afterwards.

Come on yer bastard said Mike under his breath, he'd been sweating for a full house for 8 numbers now. He only needed two fat drag queens 88 and he'd win the £500 first half full house. Number 9 popped up on the overhead board and a familiar voice yelled out house! Daisy Froglette a regular Friday nighter had won again! He was always lucky. He liked a gamble but wasn't always so lucky on the horses.

Cecil said come on its half time to a crestfallen Mike We'd better go over and say congratulations to her. No, you go I'll go t'bar said Mike. No don't be a bad looser come and say hello. They made their way to Daisy's table. She was sitting with her usual companion another well-loved drag queen called Allana Cardinal. Daisy saw them coming and held out a long gloved bejewelled hand to be kissed. Cecil did the honours Mike too embarrassed told Allana to budge up a bit so he could sit down. Allana being on the large side like Mike Squeezed up a bit but it left Mike with one buttock hanging over the edge of the booth seat. Congratulations Daisy said Cecil that's a nice win. Mikes furious he only wanted one number for ages. Thank you dear said Daisy, Oh I'm sorry Mike what a shame. Eye I was fooking sweating for 88 like. You can buy me a pint if yer like wit winnings. Daisy pretending not to have heard, (drag queens didn't think they should buy drinks on the whole) said so Cecil are you lot up at Queens

Crescent having your annual bash as usual? Yes, said Cecil, its Kris and Karl's turn to set the theme, it's going to be Hollywood's Golden Era this year. Oh, that sound fab said Allana that cow Kristallnacht has said nothing to me has she you Daisy? Oh, they will said Cecil, we are all planning what to wear now. Mike suddenly bored said I'm going t'bar what you 'aving Cec...before he could finish Daisy said I'll have a large Brandy and Port please Mike, and I'll have a pint of Stella with a Jägermeister in it please dear said Allana. Mike was effing and jeffing as he made his way to the bar.

At number 8 Olly closed his laptop with a sigh of relief, the weekend could start now. He had been working on a complicated website design for a new restaurant chain that was starting up and he was bombarded with demands from the new chains boss and was feeling a bit stressed. He went over to the fridge and poured himself a glass of white wine. First of the week and the first mouthful went down a treat. Carrying his glass upstairs he stripped off his jeans and shirt and turned the shower on in their en suite bathroom. Will had got a regular client coming around in about an hour. A corporate boss who was happy to pay double fee for a 4 hand massage with a happy ending. The client was a married "straight" professional type with a huge cock who Will quite fancied so Olly was happy to let Will issue the happy ending, while Olly stayed up the top end looking dreamily into the client's eyes while he played with his nipples. This had an extra benefit it made the client reach ecstasy levels extremely quickly, saved on body oil and they could get it over with quickly.

By the time Olly had made his way downstairs in his

Aussie bum briefs, showing off his bubble butt to perfection the client George had already arrived. He'd already undressed and was using the downstairs shower while Will similarly attired as Olly was rolling out a clean towel on the massage bed. Olly streamed some relaxing music from his I phone to the sound system and dimmed the lights.

George strolled into the room with a white towel around his waist. Hey Olly, you're a sight for sore eyes man, well you both are, I've had a rough week and my back is in knots so I'm looking forward to this.

On the bed said Wills we will soon have you sorted out. I hope so said George I've promised to take the wife's sister and her husband out for dinner later, her brother in law is a right big headed twat who gets right on my tits, so I need to be calm.

45 minutes later and a very relaxed and happy George was getting dressed. Thanks lads see you in two weeks' time, book me in Will please. Sure, thing mate good to see you again. Take care and don't thump the brother in law said Olly. I'll try my best guys said George as he made his way to his new E class Mercedes.

Waving him off from the door in their dressing gowns, Olly said nice old boy, isn't he? Yeah, he's really sexy too said Will, I hope I look like that when I'm 42. You'll look even sexier said Olly cupping Wills right buttock with his hand. Will shut the door and looked into his eyes. Upstairs you now! Olly laughing said, I've got to work tonight, and you've promised to come down to the pub to see The Royal Sisters. I will, but you don't start until 8.30 and they won't be on until 10 we've got plenty of time, come on. Olly never one needing to be asked twice followed him up the stairs.

At number 4, Alistair and Renaldo were sitting at the dining table mopping up a delicious starter of pil pil garlic prawns with some home baked crusty bread. Oh, the garlic said Renaldo we will be breathing over everyone tonight they will run a mile.

Have you thought any more about our little trip to Spain with Mike and Cecil? Said Alistair. Yes, I have, and I think wc should go, but I don't want to spend 7 days in Benidorm. I would like to go and see the family first in Valencia. That sounds nice said Alistair, do you mean a few days in Valencia and then drive down to Beni to meet the boys.? Yes, I think so, there's a few new exhibitions on at the Feria centre I'd like to see, plus I want to go and check out the El Greco paintings at the Museo del Patriarch. Sounds good to me said Alistair. We can do that, there's a few restaurants I want to check out too. It seems Valencia is giving Barcelona a run for its money in the gastronomic stakes now as well as in the architectural ones. It sure is said Renaldo, its uber trendy now, even Ben and Gordon are talking about going this year and you know what a pair of snobs they are. Oh yes laughed Alistair I mentioned to Gordon that we maybe going to Benidorm at Easter and he visibly winced. Silly queen said Renaldo. She thinks Spain starts and ends in Sitges. Or in a sling in the Yumbo centre in Gran Canaria said Alistair. Renaldo giggled; I know they go all that way to lay in the dark. They both laughed.

What's next? said Renaldo wiping his mouth with his linen napkin. Merluza baked in white wine and chorizo sausage with new potatoes and broccoli spears. Delicioso, mi amor, well you've got apple crumble and custard after said Alistair. Yummy said Renaldo, the one thing you Spanish are not very good at are puddings said Alistair. I won't be able to move said Renaldo, well you will have to move I've booked a taxi at 9pm, we promised to go and see the Royal Sisters tonight Alistair said. Oh, do we have to? I've got loads of papers to mark and I'm really tired. Said Renaldo. You can do them in the morning it will do us good to go out for a change said Alistair placing a big steaming plate of hake in front of Renaldo.

Over at No2 Roz had her feet up watching the women's football on catchup. She had just forced down a vegan Quorn and butter bean curry and thought she might explode. She was a big supporter of Brighton and Hove Albion's WFC and had tickets for the Tuesday night match against Crystal Palace.

Suddenly she leapt into the air as Rianna Jarrett put one in the back of the net. GO yelled Roz, Yolanda jumped out of her skin shouted for fucks sake Roz, sorry love said Roz. You'll give me a bloody heart attack one of these days said Yo. Roz sat down on the sofa next to Yo and threw her arm around her neck and gave her a peck on the cheek. Sorry baby you know I love you.

I love you too said Yo, but do you have to be so loud! What's that you're looking at buying now? said Roz. Well I really like the look of this Yurt said Yo thumbing through the Vegans Weekly. What another one? said Roz. Well I thought if we moved the old one further down the garden, I could use that for my yoga and meditation, and if we bought this one or two maybe, we could offer air B&B for other lesbian

22

or trans women, looking for a peaceful retreat. If we put them up nearer to the back door, they could use the downstairs loo and shower or maybe you could build an outside one where we could recycle all the rainwater. It would soon pay for itself.

Oh, I don't know hun, I don't get in now until after 3am I can't get up and start looking after guests said Roz. No, we can make the Yurts self-catering, maybe solar powered electric rings to boil water or cook some oats said Yo. A fresh fruit basket, cereal, soya milk that sort of thing. I'm thinking just June until September, Mainly the school holidays, I'm off for weeks I'll have time. We can put the money towards that adventure holiday you keep on about said Yo looking at Roz with that sweet little angelic look she saved for when she wanted to get her own way. Roz melting said oh alright, one Yurt give it a go then, but it's your gig Yo I want nothing to do with it ok? Of course, said Yo smiling sweetly.

I'm just going up to get changed Yo. Ok don't forget you promised we would go down to the Fawcett Inn to see the Royal Sisters tonight before you go to work. Did I, oh God do you really want to go? Yes, we said we'd support the boys, they've put a new number in the act apparently said Yo, about time said Roz they've been doing the same old shit since the 1970's. It's a new Dusty Springfield Medley said Yo, oh bang up to date then laughed Roz. Well they can hardly do the pussy cat dolls at their age can they said Yo. No mores the pity thought Roz. What she'd like to do to Nicole Scherzinger was nobody's business. Anyway, said Yo, Dusty s a lesbian Icon, a true feminist not like those tarts exploiting their sexuality, making women look like trash just for heterosexual

23

men to masturbate over, disgusting! Right I'm going up! Want to get in the shower with me Yo? Said Roz thoughts of the pussy cat dolls making her get a little warm in her hidden place. No, you're alright said Yo, I'm gonna freeze the rest of this Quorn curry for you for dinner next week when I'm in London at a meeting for our new protest group Extinction Rebellion. It's going to be great we will bring London to a standstill very soon Yo said excitedly. Great said Roz with as much enthusiasm she could muster. She'd put it out for the seagulls and pop down to Wetherspoons for a nice juicy steak instead.

Down at the Fawcett Inn Frank was down in the cellar lining some barrels up for the Friday night onslaught and doing some bottle sorting while it was quiet. Josh was behind the bar chatting to a few guys left over from the 6 o'clock session. They always did well on the happy hour between 5pm and 7pm. People would pop in after work to relax before going home, Friday night some just stayed on until closing time. There was a nice atmosphere, the lighting was fairly dark, so some guys were cruising each other a bit. Others sat looking at their phones and a few jolly queens sat at the bar dishing the dirt with Josh. Can we have another round please Josh said Tina Tits one of the regulars, real name Terry, about 60 but had man boobs so Josh had nicknamed him Tina tits and it had stuck. Two house double gin and tonics, 2 pints of Stella and a Perrier water please dear.

Who's the Perrier for then? Said Josh. Oh Larry Allcock he's just come in. Got a dose again can't drink dear said Tina tits. Bloody hell not again said Josh has he never heard of condoms? He says he can't get any to fit. Bollocks said Josh, no its true said Tina. I saw it in the cottage once. Like a baby's arm holding and orange dear. They don't call him Allcock for nothing said Tina (Larry's real name was Pierce) I always thought it was socks down there said Josh, that packets not natural at all. Do you want lemon or lime, said Josh? Lemon please dear. Hello Larry, here's your Perrier love. Thanks Tina said Larry, only one more night to go and I'll have finished the course. You really should be more careful you know Larry said Tina, HIV may not be a death risk like it was in my day dear, but you can still catch it. I know I know but I get fed up with wanking said Larry. Well I can always take me teeth out and give you a blowie dear. Thanks, but no thanks said Larry, suit yerself said Tina. That'll be £15.80 please Tina said Josh. We'll have one yourself and ask Mary if she wants one said Tina. Mary Barley was the barmaid/manager, she was up on a chair cleaning off the top shelves while it was quiet. Mary do you want a drink with Tina? said Josh. Thanks lurve I'll have £2 worth darlin, I'll have it later, when I've finished. I might as well get pissed, I'm not gonna get fooked am I, well not in 'ere anyway. They all laughed Mary always said the same thing and it always made them laugh.

Frank and Josh had inherited Mary Barley when they took over the pub. She had worked there for 25 years and knew everyone. Josh really liked her and thought she'd be an asset which she was. She lived above the pub and was on the licence with Frank and Josh. She was quite capable of running the pub if they went on holiday. She was a diamond. Originally from St Helens in Lancashire, she had had a hard life. A single mum who had taken any job going until she had landed in Brighton aged 30. She applied for a job at The Fawcett Inn, she didn't know what a gay pub was then, but she soon learnt. Open minded by nature she took everything as it came and didn't care who did what to who. She said exactly what she thought and took no prisoners. She was glamorous in a way, she had a penchant for animal prints and gold jewellery, high heels and faux fur coats. Peter the previous landlord had been there years and took her on because she made him laugh and she had stayed ever since. Part of Brighton folklore she had become a bit of a legend. Her only fault was her language. Josh had tried to stop her swearing but it didn't last long. One night she said I got so pissed last night dear, to a customer and Josh kicked her gently and said language! What language said Mary? Pissed said Josh, say you were merry or a bit worse for wear. Oh, I'm sorry lurve said Mary I didn't know piss was a swear word lurve. Josh gave up after that and let her get on with it. Which she did at every opportunity.

Frank came up from the cellar and said, I'll just go over and check the sound and lighting for the stage, you know what the Royal Sisters are like, think they are still working the Palladium. Better put some fookin Vaseline on them lights too lurve, shouted out Mary at their age they'll need all the fookin help they can get. Making everyone in the pub start laughing.

Back at No7 Karl and Kris were preparing for the nights show. They prepared in different ways. Once they had been to the huge summer house in their garden which contained all their frocks and Karl's sewing machine and props, picked out their dresses and wigs for the evening performance and loaded the car. Karl liked to lay down in the dark on top of the bed and watch an old film and relax.

Kris liked to pour a large gin and tonic and vocalise for an hour warming his throat up. Kris still had a good voice despite the gin and the fags. First, he would select a CD to get him in the mood. A big fan and friend of the late Dorothy Squires, Dorothy live at the London Palladium which Kris had seen as a young lad was a good mood raiser. Then he would start the make-up. This was a labour of love. He had been taught how to make up by one of the best in the business and he was a master with the eyebrow pencil and blusher. To do the whole face or "eke" as they called it took one hour. He changed from an ageing sixty something Cliff Richard type into a stunning Hollywood star of yesteryear a real beauty his favourite Joan Crawford. A tight headband and a chinstrap taking years off of him. Once he had stood in front of the mirror channelling "la Squires" while Dorothy took round after round of applause, Kris was ready.

Next, he would pop into Karl's room, (they had long had separate bedrooms) and get to work on Karl's eke. This didn't take as long as Karl had been under the surgeon's knife several times. Kris had only had an eye lift and was saving up for a neck lift as It had taken years off of his dear friend Barbara Windsor.

Karl eyed himself up in the mirror. Thanks dear you've done a bona job, he pulled on his matching track suit the same as Kris's and took a swig of Kris's Gin. Jesus Kris did you put any tonic in that at all dear? Just a whisper said Kris.

They made their way downstairs and out to the car. They didn't give a shit driving through Brighton in full slap, in fact they loved it when they stopped at the lights and peered in at the drivers who had pulled along beside them. The looks on some of the faces had them both in stitches. They could only afford this luxury if they were performing locally. Usually it was the ladies toilet in some back street pub with a bare light bulb and a cracked mirror. Pulling up outside the Fawcett Inn, Karl whipped his mother's blue disabled badge out of the glove compartment and placed it on the dashboard. A necessity in Brighton because the council hated motorists. Then once unpacked they entered the pub, wigs in one hand frocks in the other and glided regally through the bar to Marys flat upstairs to "prepare"

Back down in the bar the pub was starting to get busy. The bingo gang had made their way down from Freshfield Road and were piling in the door. Daisy Froglett and Allana pulled up in a taxi, looking like the Queen Mother and lady in waiting attending a premiere. When they entered the bar, Daisy made her way to her favourite stool at the bar and pulled the young queen sitting on it off by his ear. Hello Mary, dear said Daisy. A large Brandy and port for me and a Pint of Stella with a Jägermeister in it for Allana.

Ello Daisy lurve any luck at the bingo? Said Mary. Eye he did, got the £500 first t'house said Mike as he squeezed in at the bar next to Allana. £500 ooo lovely said Mary. Drinks all round then is it Daisy? Daisy pretending not to hear picked up a menu from the bar and studied it studiously. Allana looked at her nails. £14.80 please said Mary putting the drinks in front of them. Can I put it on a tab dear said Daisy I'll Pay you at the end. Mary muttered something under her breath and said to Mike right what you 'avin lurve?

Daisy got bought a lot of drinks, which he put in the bin (in credit) so hopefully by the end of the night he wouldn't owe a penny.

Mike and Cecil joined Alistair and Renaldo on a table near the front of the stage, Alistair and Renaldo had got there early to save a table. Yolanda was on a high stool near the back watching Roz thrash this young hipster type, long beard skinny jeans, tight shirt, at the pool table. She kept an eye out as Roz didn't think much to the hipster types calling them pretentious bastards and she might lash out if she didn't win. More people poured through the door, and it was all go behind the bar. Olly had come on duty looking flushed but happy and the four of them were serving non-stop behind the bar. Frank said keep that till ringing boys and girls its better than an orgasm. I've forgotten what that is said Mary. Olly hasn't have you love said Josh with a grin. Olly winked at Josh. Twice actually he grinned. I'm surprised you can walk said Frank. Don't assume said Olly. Will standing at the bar said. Oy do you mind.

Tina Tits, Larry Allcock and two others had progressed from the bar to a table at the front too. Larry had elbowed the Perrier water and was knocking back pints of Kronenberg. Tina now a bit sloshed he'd been there since 6pm was getting a bit loud and waving his arms about a bit. Larry said slow down a bit mate, Oh I'm alright dear said Tina, mothers' milk to me.

Frank pushed a button behind the bar and the show medley overture came on. 10 minutes of show song highlights to get everyone in the mood for the cabaret. Upstairs Kris drained his third large gin, took a deep breath and followed Karl a teeny bit wobbly down the stairs. Taking deep breaths, they stood at the bottom of the stairs ready to take to the stage. Frank made his way to the stage, a big drum roll sounded and said Ladies and Gentlemen, and the stage lights came up. Welcome to the Fawcett Inn on this lovely Friday night. Tonight, we have one of your favourite acts, stars of the west end and Las Vegas please put your hands together for the one and only Royal Sisters. John Bishon the talented pianist and keyboard player struck up the opening introduction to "sisters" the boys opening song. Karl and Kris grabbed their microphones and launched into "Sisters never where their such devoted sisters"

Over at number 5 Ben and Gordon were in full leather fetish gear. Gordon had on a fetish puppy gimp mask and a leather collar onto which Ben had attached a leather lead. He also wore a leather harness and leather shorts wrist and ankle cuffs.

Ben was more traditional in leather chaps and a leather waistcoat.

The door rang and the first two guests had arrived, Gordon barked when the doorbell rang, then made whimpering noises as Ben opened the door to let them in. A couple who they had played with before and knew the score. Patting Gordon on the head and offering him a doggie treat from out of their pockets, they made their way through to the kitchen diner where they were offered drinks. Fifteen minutes later the doorbell went again, and Gordon scampered to the door on all fours whimpering and barking. Down boy yelled Ben and Sit! Gordon squatted down on to his haunches obediently. Ben opened the door to this Guy who was new on the scene and they hadn't met him before. A tall stocky man stood there, Good looking in a rough way, pockmarked skin and a scar down his right cheek. He also had very thick lensed glasses on, which accentuated his dark brown almost black eyes. Hi, I'm Bill said the guest extending his hand to Ben. Ben went to shake it, but Gordon was off again whimpering and jumping up and trying to lick Bills hand. Down boy said Ben and pulled the lead in tight. Hi Bill come in and have a drink. Thanks, said Bill. Lively little thing isn't he.

Making their way through to the kitchen, Ben introduced Bill to the other two. Peter and Paul and said, beer scotch or red wine Bill? I'll have a scotch on the rock's thanks said Bill.

Ben whistled and pointed to Gordon who knew the cue and got into his basket under the table.

After some initial chit chat. Ben opened a drawer and got out some cocaine. A client he was trying to save from deportation who had been convicted for drugs crimes had put him in touch with a top dealer working the county lines in Sussex. He only supplied grade A gear and Ben only liked the best. Chopping up several lines of Charlie, he offered it around to the others. Paul and Peter dived in with relish. Bill snorted a few lines then said, I can roll a spliff if you like I've got some great hash. Ben said sorry under no circumstances whatsoever do we allow tobacco products or smoking in this part of the house, but if you want to indulge when we get into the dungeon feel free, as long as you blow the smoke in the dogs face and use him as an ashtray ill allow it. Ben was always the same when he snorted coke. It brought out a side to him normally buried to the public. Underneath the liberal woke persona he displayed at work and socially, he was a cruel sadistic bastard with lots of pent up anger. With pleasure said Bill staring under the table at Gordon who was trembling with fear and anticipation. Ben passed a couple of lines of Charlie on a slate under the table with a straw for Gordon.

After a few more lines of Coke and another drink the groups confidence rose, and the banter got louder.

Are we all ready to give this silly bitch under the table a good seeing to then shouted Ben?

Yes, shouted the others bring it on. Dragging Gordon out from under the table, Ben said follow me, and the others followed him up to the dungeon.

Right at the top of the house there was a large master bedroom with an en suite bathroom that Ben and Gordon had converted into their dungeon. What was once a chic modern, luxury space had been turned into a horror chamber. Reinforced walls and ceiling, false floor and every inch completely soundproofed. The window had been blocked up from the inside and a ventilation unit installed. The room ran the entire length of the house including the bathroom. Every wall was painted black or mirrored. The ceiling was mirrored. Even the bathroom had been painted black. On one wall were several shelves containing their vast amount of equipment and toys. Every type of whip and restraint gadget you can imagine was attached to the wall.

Pride of place was the sling. Designed in Germany it could be moved around by remote control and highered and lowered too. Bill looked around impressed. Stripping their clothes off down to jock straps the guys lifted Gordon and manoeuvred him into the sling. Strapping him in tight. They positioned themselves at various points around the sling. Ben opened up a huge pot of Crisco and offered it around. Bill lit up the spliff. He blew the smoke straight into Gordon's face, showing him the red hot end. With his glasses off Bill looked more viscous than before, like a villain, a tall Bob Hoskins. Gordon underneath the mask said rather nervously my safe word is, Tupperware. Bill laughed and spat in Gordon's face and said What's a safe word?

The Dusty Springfield medley had gone down a treat at the Fawcett Inn. The Royal Sisters were closing the first half of their act, they were pleased with the response. Although they were giving daggers to Tina tits who now over emotional and tired kept yelling go Dusty, and wept all the way through "You don't have to say you love me" As they left the stage for the break they swept through the audience, Karl stooping to whisper into Tina ear. Shut the fuck up for the second half or we'll annihilate you, you stupid old queen alright? Tina looked dumbstruck. Smiling and waving to all they retreated upstairs to Marys flat where there was a tray of drinks waiting for them.

Well that went down well eh? said Kris pouring himself out a large Gin, yes great except for that silly cow Tina in the front said Karl, any more of that and I'll do the old spit in the drink routine. You know ask for a sip as, I'm so dry then gob in it and hand it back.

Kris laughed; it's been a few years since we've done that. Do you remember at the Vauxhall tavern years ago, we always did it to that lot remember? Yers well they was always fucking heckling in there wasn't they, rowdy bunch of cunts they were, said Karl slipping into pure cockneyese now they were alone. Kris slipped his high heels off and sat on Marys sofa.

Look at this flat dear said Kris, Marys certainly gone to town in ere 'asnt she. Well if you like early Jewish sneered Karl. Its ok but all that clutter and those gold mirrors takes a bit of dusting. I like the way she s draped the leopard skin rugs over the chairs though said Kris, might be a bit OTT but she's got a bona eye. Oh, yers she as I'll give 'er that. She told me she's up at the crack of dawn on a Sunday morning to get on Brighton market, she goes up there with no makeup on and a scarf round her head. Looks like a bleedin bag lady, that way she can get a bargain. Well she's right said Kris, no point going up there done up to the nines is it dear, they'd double the price. Kris reached for the gin bottle; do you want a little one dear? No, I'd better not I'm driving I'll 'ave a couple when we get 'ome. and you'd better not 'ave anymore either dear. I'm channelling Dorothy Squires said Kris. Yes, well even she didn't go on legless dear. Oh, shut up said Kris, come on text Frank downstairs and tell him 5 minutes I'll just go for a slash.

The second half went down even better than the first. They opened together with "There's no business like show business" which set Daisy Froglette off into a rant, saying that's my opening number the pair of cockney cows. Then they went into their solo numbers. Kris did a mean Judy Garland doing Get happy and The man that got away, he'd worked hard on the leg work and draping the microphone chord over his shoulder as he moved his way around the stage, clutching his throat and tipping his head back for the big note at the end. Tina despite the warning was on his feet clapping and crying at the same time, but to be fair so was everyone. Then Karl came on as Mae West in a fabulous mermaid gown and a huge hat singing, "I'm in the mood for love"

Alistair came back from the bar with a round of drinks for their table, pass these over to Cecil and Mike Renaldo please. Renaldo stared right through him in a world of his own, Renaldo please said Alistair I'll drop this tray in a minute. Mike stood up and relieved Alistair of the heavy tray. Renaldo coming to said sorry I was miles away. Truth was Renaldo was dreaming about getting away on holiday, he liked the Fawcett Inn, but it was the same every weekend and the continual rain outside was getting him down.

The Encore which was expected came after much yelling for more and bravos, downing the last of his drink, Kris joined hands with Karl as they made their way back on to the stage. The finale featured the two of them sitting alone in front of a wheeled on dressing room mirror with lights around the edges, miming to the legendary Larry Paulette singing Charles Aznavour's What makes a man a man. Slowly removing all signs of makeup and removing their dresses to strip down to tights and underpants they ended on the last bit of the song by both pulling off their wigs simultaneously and starring into the ether defiantly. The cheers and applause went on forever. Even Daisy said to Allana See that's what people want a bit of fucking nostalgia. Yes, well they haven't got much choice with you, dear, have they? Daisy glared as Allana downed her sixth pint of Stella.

At number 5 things were in full sling. Each of the men had taken it in turns to humiliate and torture the puppy hanging before them. A lot of the toys from the shelf had been used well. Gordon getting extremely uncomfortable now, was hoping the session was coming to an end. He wondered if the guys would take off his mask for a bukkake ending, he did hope so, however, Bill had other ideas he wasn't finished yet. As he reached down for the Crisco pot, he reached out and grabbed a large metallic object from the shelf.

The Royal Sisters took their finale bows before making their way backstage to recover. Bona show slurred Kris, yes dear said Karl thought you were going to fall into the pit at the end there dear, come on let's get upstairs grab our stuff and make our way home, shall we? Spoilsport said Kris. As they made their way through the bar too much, back slapping and complements. Frank shoved the nights fee in Karl's hand and said thanks mate you were great. The boys went upstairs changed into their lemon tracksuits and slipped out of the side door. I can't wait to get in and have a proper bevy said Karl, I need to wind down after that show I'm so up.

When they got back to Queens Crescent, they emptied the car and dumped their stuff in the hall. Leave it Kris I'll sort it in the morning. Go and pour me a drink will you a large one please dear. Coming up said Kris opening the freezer to get out the ice cubes.

He slipped on a CD of show tunes and they settled on the sofa ready to do the post-mortem, go over in detail their show and relive together how wonderful they had been.

The Fawcett Inn stayed busy for another hour or so. Alistair and Renaldo gave Mike and Cecil a lift home. Mike invited them in for a night cap. Come in and we'll talk about us 'olidays. You can't 'ear yerself fooking talk downt pub. Ok why not said Alistair.

They made their way into Cecil and Mikes lounge. It was quite grand in fact it resembled the lounge area in their hotel in Blackpool. Some nice antique tables and lamps, some reproduction gold framed paintings on the walls Two big cream leather sofas and a huge leather recliner for Mike. Renaldo thought the red flock wallpaper on the feature wall was something his granny in Spain would have loved. Cecil came back from the kitchen with a large ice bucket and opened up the front of a large reproduction cocktail cabinet, full of beautiful crystal glasses and every type of spirit you could think of. Renaldo and Alistair very happily accepted two generous single malt whiskeys and Cecil poured two large vodkas and tonics no ice for him and Mike.

We've decided to go out to Valencia for a few days first said Alistair. Renaldo wants to go and visit his family and visit a few of the art galleries, and I want to go to some of the new restaurants I've heard about.

Oh, that'll be nice said Cecil I like Valencia we went there for the day didn't we Mike when we were staying at the Don Pancho hotel in Benidorm years ago. Yes, we did ages ago said Mike. Nice place but there was some sort of fiesta going on. Fooking fireworks blasting and all these statues burning in the street. Oh, that will be the Falla's in March said Renaldo. Que espectacular! my grandmother lives near the main square and every year she has to have to have her windows replaced with the glass, it used to break because of the sound. I remember said Mike I couldn't ear owt for fooking days afterwards. Yes, well the rep gave you earplugs to wear and you wouldn't wear them, so it was your own fault said Cecil. So, you'll come down to Benidorm afterwards?

said Mike. Yes, we will hire a car at the airport and drive down to meet you. Will you book the hotel for us Mike? Said Alistair. Oh, eye no problemo there mate. Phillipe The Duchess of Benidorm is a good mate of ours, I told 'im you were coming too. He's booked us two nice rooms at the Casa don Phillipe. You'll fooking luv it. He's a right card is Phillipe. Very funny, wait till you see 'I'm doing play yer cards right after midnight.

Play your cards, right? Said Renaldo, yes, it's an old English TV show from way back with Bruce Forsyth said Cecil its hilarious.

Alistair was wondering what he had let himself in for but said enthusiastically. I can't wait! I'm a Benidorm virgin. You won't be one for long said Mike laughing not when we take you to GG's bar int old town.

What's that said Alistair. It's a drinking club for the older gentlemen and their admirer's like us. There's a big bar quite dark with a dance floor, then there's a lounge area with pool tables and sofas, a cinema where they show porno films. Then out back there's a dark room if you want to cop off like. And then next to that some cabins with locks ont door. Me and Cec go there every night. Do you really said Renaldo every night? Well most nights said Mike. We meet this Spanish geezer over there Paco, about thirty he is, married, 4 kids, int closet like, but ee loves a bit of cock, loves being fooked. We take it in turns, one night I go oop top end and Cecil goes downt bottom end, then next night I go downt bottom end and Cecil goes oop top like.

Alistair gasped. Cecil going bright red and dimpling said really Mike do you have to go into so much detail honestly. Oh, shut up you daft cont, were all men 'ere together aren't we? Said Mike. Renaldo Said, oh yes in Spain there are clubs like that. There is no stigma about age. Older men are considered attractive and wise. Plus, lots of catholic men who are bi use these clubs for sex and male company. A lot of the wives know but they look the other way as it gives them a break.

What are the restaurants like said Alistair beetroot red and changing the subject? Oh, great said Mike. There's all sorts. Lots of fabulous tapas bars said Cecil, streets of them, sometimes I can persuade Mike to go. I do try now and then said Mike some of its all reet but to be honest I'm 'appy to go to Rays fish and chips shop, they do the best haddock and chips with curry sauce this side of Manchester. Sounds delightful said Alistair. Oh, it is lovely said Cecil. Lots of bars, dead cheap, and gorgeous beaches its beautiful in the old town. We've been going there now for over 20 years said Mike. Do you go anywhere else other times of the year? Said Renaldo. No point said Mike. Why would we? said Cecil looking puzzled.

Last orders at the bar yelled Josh as he rang the bell. Most people had left to go home or go on to a late bar, but there were a few stragglers left. Mary was going around wiping the tables and laughing with some of the older customers she had known for years. Good night eh said Frank squeezing Josh's bum. Yeah great but my feet are killing me and I'm ready to go home. Olly was just emptying the glass machine said to Will I'll drive home, we'll give you a lift Yo, you've both had a few wines I've only had one. Nooo I'll be fine on my bike said Yo, no forget your carbon footprint for once said Olly I'll drive, push your bike around the back of the pub. Brighton doesn't need another dyke on a bike on a Friday night especially a pissed one. Honestly, your language Olly, it's so retro and sexist to say dyke ugh! Yeah whatever Greta Thunderfuck drink up. Will laughed, you know Olly's not woke yet Yo. No, he sure isn't, I'll enlighten him one day.

Frank had sent Mary up to her flat as she looked a bit tired and he had let Olly go with Yo and Will. They had locked up and were just cashing up and doing the till when they thought they heard a noise coming from downstairs. Did you hear that said Josh? I heard something said Frank. Stay here I'll go down and have a look. Be careful said Josh handing Frank a Mallett they kept under the bar just in case.

Frank made his way downstairs; the cellar was down there next to the toilets. He checked in there first and nothing. Then he heard a groan and pushed back the door of the gents, nothing there. He checked the lock up, nothing. He opened the door of the ladies and there was Tina Tits on her knees giving Larry Allcock the blow job of his life. What the fuck do you think you two are up to down here said Frank. Come on out the pair of yer! Hang on mate said a very drunk Larry I haven't finished yet, I couldn't give a shit said Frank, out the pair of you. Larry withdrew his member and tried to put it back in his jeans but was struggling. Franks eyes popped out on stalks; he'd seen some big ones in the army but nothing like that. I can do you too Frank while I've got me teeth out slurred Tina. No thanks said Frank I'm not that fucking desperate, I am said Larry, fucking charming said Tina. Come on get up said Frank I can't said Tina you'll have to help. Come on

Larry help me get the old slag up the stairs, I'm not an old slag you horrible bastard said Tina as they dragged him up the stairs, I'm just a girl who can't say no! Then laughing at his own joke. Started singing with gusto the hit song from Oklahoma. He was still singing it as Josh held open the front door and Frank pushed them both out into the street. Locking the door Josh looked at Frank and said Well! Then they both burst out laughing. Come on let's get the fuck out of here said Frank.

Most of the residents of Queens Crescent were home or having night caps when they heard a police siren going off. Cecil looked out of the window and said to the others, oh fuck an ambulance is pulling up outside of Ben and Gordon's. Mike Alistair and Renaldo made their way to the window to see what was going on.

Two paramedics made their way into number 5, after quickly assessing the situation they said, it's a trip to the hospital for you Mr. Oh no said Ben can't you help him here? No sorry this is beyond our remit; this guy needs to be seen straight away. The paramedics made their way back out to the ambulance to get a stretcher. Ben looked furiously at Gordon, trust you! How do you think this is going to look for me if this gets out? I'm sorry Ben, I kept trying to yell "Tupperware", but I couldn't make myself understood as my mouth was full at the time. Idiot said Ben. The Paramedics came back in with the stretcher got it on the bedroom floor and lifted the embarrassed and weeping Gordon onto the stretcher. They covered his naked body with a blanket the best they could to shield his modesty. Will you come in the ambulance with your friend sir? Ben said no I'll lock up and follow down in the car.

As the paramedics lifted Gordon up and made their way down the stairs to the front door, Ben scooted around to make sure there was no signs of drugs anywhere, put a padlock on the dungeon door and checked the back door was locked. The others when they realised the danger of the situation had quickly got dressed, stripped Gordon of his fetish gear and mask and helped Ben carry him downstairs to the bedroom, then fled ASAP.

By now the other residents had gathered on the green opposite to watch the goings on. Oh, I do hope no one's died said Cecil getting emotional. Na it'll be allreet said Mike, come ere ya daft cont said Mike pulling Cecil towards him lovingly, with his arm around his shoulder. Alistair a bit flustered said to Renaldo I wonder if they need any help. Stop panicking Alistair wait and see what's happened said Renaldo. John and Grant came over and said what's going on? The kids from number 8 ran over with coats on over their boxers causing the others a quandary of where to look first the accident scene or at their packets.

At number 7 Karl had passed out on top of his bed exhausted, they had sat up for an hour and a half reliving the show and telling each other how marvellous they had been. They had polished off nearly a litre bottle of gin between them. Stripping down to their G string briefs, they were unwinding by dancing and doing high kicks around the sitting room to the soundtrack of a Chorus line. Karl said that's it I'm pissed I'm off to bed Kris. Ok I'll be up shortly said Kris, refilling his glass with the last of the gin, selected Dorothy Squires live at Drury Lane and slumped onto the sofa, passing out within minutes, It was the commotion and the flashing lights outside that woke him, stumbling to the window he said aloud what the fuck, staggered to the sitting room door and into the hall and grabbed a coat off of the coat hook, slipped on some shoes, opened the door and staggered up to number 5 to see what was going on.

There was an audible gasp from the others then a bit of laughing, Kris in his haste had grabbed the Dougie Darnell Dorothy Squires Ostrich feather cape by mistake and was staggering up to the ambulance with the front wide open in 6 inch heels. What the fuck does she look like said Grant. Like a Canary that's been in the pussy cat's mouth said Renaldo. Look something's happening said Yolanda wrapped in a Tibetan poncho, topped off with a blue and yellow star euro beret. The others looked over, just then Gordon was coming out feet first, knees up in a stirrup position. As the paramedics turned him to manoeuvre him into the ambulance. Kris who was hanging onto the door got blinded by a powerful light, temporarily blinded lost his footing and fell sideways into a low hedge. We haven't got time to help you as well Mrs said the driver, Its Miss! yelled an indignant Kris legs sticking out of the bush.

When the ambulance started to pull away Ben came out and locked the door. The others made their way over concerned. John and Grant pulled a stroppy Kris from the hedge, He fucking pushed me that bloke said Kris, yeah of course he did "miss" laughed Grant. What's happened Ben said Cecil? Can we help in anyway said Alistair? Suspected heart failure said Ben but he's ok, he's safe they are just taking him in to check him over properly. Oh, poor Gordon said Alistair do give him our love. If there's anything we can do said Yolanda let us know. Thanks everyone said Ben getting emotional. I do hope his heart will be ok. Heart my arse muttered Kris, now hanging onto Mikes arm to steady himself, looked like the Blackpool illuminations from where I was standing.

Gordon was whipped into A&E at the Royal Sussex county hospital, put on a trolley and wheeled into a cubicle where a large framed African nurse called Chandice pulled a curtain quickly around the bed. What ave you been up to den? said Nurse Chandice with a delightful Jamaican lilt. Gordon in pain and deeply embarrassed pointed downwards. Nurse Chandice lifting the blanket looked down and gasped. Oh, my Lord oh my Goodness I never ever seen a thing like dat! Oh, my goodness, not ever, no. Peering over the top of the blanket she said how did dat thing get in dere then eh? I slipped on the stairs said Gordon. Slipped on the stairs? Said Chandice. Is you telling me the truth boy? I don't think so, no way! Standing upright she stuck her head out from the curtain and called to the nurse opposite. Bernadette, Bernadette. What? said Bernie a middle age old hand from Dublin, come 'ere and see what de batty boy did do! Said Chandice.

Bernadette came over, took one look under the blanket, sighed then crossed herself. Fell on de stairs den did you? Why Yes said Gordon I was coming down from the top floor when I lost my..... Save it for the doctor dear said Bernie, she'd seen it all before, lightbulbs, milk bottles, garden equipment, hoover attachments. Mother Celesta hadn't warned her of any of this when she'd left the convent. Nurse Chandice had another peek under the blanket giggled, said I'll get the Doctor. Hurry! said Gordon. Dont worry dear, doze batteries last forever guffawed Chandice, singing "light up light up" as she made her way to the desk to call for the emergency Doctor.

Gordon had needed surgery, Bill when reaching out in the dark had made a mistake and grabbed the large torch, a flashlight voyager with rubber finish it was incredibly thick and ten inches long so any easy mistake to make. With the Cocaine and the poppers, he'd got carried away and shoved it in too far. The Doctor tried with forceps, but he couldn't get a grip with the amount of Crisco lubricant still attached. He, Nurses Chandice and Bernadette got Gordon in all sorts of positions but to no avail. Bernie kept saying breathe, that's it, now Push! it'll come out in a minute. Dr Prajapati said exasperated, nurse we are conducting an extraction of a foreign body not inducing childbirth. Sorry Dr said Bernie.

The next morning Gordon was back on the recovery ward, when he woke up, the first flashback came and he groaned in horror as well as pain, He buried his face in the pillow and wept with humiliation. A new nurse came by and stopped at his bed, are you ok? No cried Gordon. Would you like some tea said Romeo, a delightful Filipino nurse from Manila. Yes, please said Gordon, do you have organic milk? Yeah sure laughed Romeo and went to fetch the tea. Gordon eventually sat himself up in the bed and drank his tea, He knew everyone must know his shame, several people passing the bed looked down and giggled as they went past. This was most embarrassing how did they know? It wasn't until Ben arrived for their meeting with the surgeon that he found out.

Ben had not gone to the hospital the night before; he drove off from the house thinking what to do. He didn't fancy sitting in A&E with Gordon whining, so still horny as he hadn't shot his load yet, he turned right onto the seafront and drove along to the cruising area in Kemp town. Here he parked up and got out for a stroll in the bushes it wasn't long before someone came along and gave him the much needed relief he required. He didn't see their face. As he was zipping up, he started to walk away, Oy! what about me? yelled the bit of trade. Go fuck yourself said Ben walking away.

Saturday morning was a quiet affair in the Crescent; however, spring was dawning, and the clocks went forward tonight so a few of the gang who were up had their French or bi folding doors open onto their gardens. The sun was shining so those who were facing east/ south were getting a long needed blast of sunshine after a particularly cold winter.

At number 4 Cecil had the frying pan out and was cooking up a delicious full English for himself and Mike, sausages, black pudding bacon, beans the full Monty. Old school they preferred a greasy breakfast after a heavy night out. I wish you hadn't have told Alistair and Renaldo about what we get up to at GG's in Benidorm said Cecil I was so embarrassed. Why? you daft bugger said Mike if we are gonna take them there they might as well know the score. Well it might not be their thing said Cecil you know how devoted they are, I can't imagine them doing anything like that. Well sometimes its quiet ones who are worst said Mike pass the brown sauce will ya. I hope poor Gordon is ok said Cecil, what a shock.

There's more to that than meets the eye said Mike. Like what said Cecil, I were down pits remember, I saw all sorts going on. It's surprising where those miners' lamps end up.

At number 6 Alistair and Renaldo were devouring a plate of Churros and hot chocolate after devouring a thick bacon sandwich each. Poor Gordon said Alistair, he's incredibly young to have a heart problem. Mmm said Renaldo, thinking, I don't think it's his heart that is breaking. Out loud he said yes let's hope he is ok, I heard Ben come home about an hour after they took Gordon to hospital so it can't have been too serious can it. I suppose not said Alistair.

At number 2 Yo was pouring some almond milk onto a bowl of organic muesli. She was sitting at the kitchen table reading her Saturday Guardian. There was an article on her new hero Greta Thunberg the autistic climate change warrior who was getting world recognition especially from the BBC and some of the press as a sort of new messiah. At 16 she was scowling at the world and telling them off for being naughty for not taking climate change seriously. Yo thought she was wonderful and couldn't wait to go to any meeting she held in England. Upstairs Roz was still in bed having not gotten in until 4 am, she'd gone with the other doorman from work to the all night diner for a gutbuster. Now she could smell the bacon frying from the surrounding houses and her mouth was watering even though she was still full. She looked at the clock 10.30 am, she rolled over and went back to sleep, she decided she couldn't face a bowl of muesli this morning.

At number 7, Karl woke up groaning, his head pounding a bit, Jesus he must start pouring his own drinks when they got in, He crossed the floor to his en suite and looked in the mirror. Oh, gawd not a pretty fucking site he said to his reflection. He looked in the bathroom cabinet no paracetamol. He cleaned his teeth pulled on a dressing gown and fluffy rabbit slippers and thought he'd go down and search for some and put the kettle on. When he opened the bedroom door, he muttered what the fuck? There staring in his face were Kris's underpants hanging from the chandelier at the top of the stairs. Looking down he could see stiletto heel shoes on different stairs and right at the bottom Dorothy Squires ostrich feather cape strewn on the floor by the front door. He looked into Kris's bedroom there he was stark naked half on the bed half off, knees on the floor with his head on the bed. On the floor was an empty gin bottle and an overturned glass.

Kris! Kris! for fuck sake wake up Karl said shaking him. What, what's the matter said Kris. Get up dear, look at the fucking state of you, honestly you never even made it into bed this time! Oh, leave me alone said Kris, Karl bent down and hurled him over onto the bed and covered him up with a dressing gown, picking another gin bottle up and dirty glass and overflowing ashtray. Tutting he decided to let him sleep it off while he went downstairs.

The others in the Crescent went about their normal business. Frank and John had already left to get down to the Fawcett arms and get the bar ready for the day ahead. John and Grant got up as usual at 7am and were out of the door by 8.00am on their way to work in Hove. The kids Olly and Will were still fast asleep they didn't usually appear much before 12 at the weekend. Ben got up and went straight onto his computer to do some work on his asylum seekers case. He worked through until about 12.30pm then decided he had better get down to the hospital to check on Gordon.

Standing at the end of Gordon's bed. Ben feeling a bit remorseful now the drugs had worn off, said how are you today? In agony said Gordon where were you last night? Oh, I decided not to drive as I had been drinking and I couldn't get a cab from anywhere. I did phone the hospital he lied to check that you were ok, so, how are you? I'm so embarrassed, said Gordon. I could murder that Bill. Oh, it wasn't really his fault, easy mistake to make said Ben, it was your fault really for not putting it back in the kitchen. Gordon just looked at him, and on top of that everyone who walks past this bed keeps laughing, who told them? that's what I want to know. Ben glancing down started to laugh, what are you laughing at said Gordon. This said Ben, holding up a piece of A4 cardboard, someone had changed the name on the bed and put a sign up saying Miss Dura Cell "Can last for up to 44 hours" Ohhhh screamed Gordon covering his face up with a pillow.

Gordon was dismissed from hospital about 2pm after a stern lecture from the duty doctor. I don't wish to judge you on your private lives and I'm well aware of the different proclivities we all have when it comes down to sexual identity and behaviours. However, there is a limit on how much strain the rectum can stand. Turning to Ben, and you as the "master" in this situation, (he actually did those annoying air quotation marks that made Ben want to punch him) need to take more care of your partner. Now no more intercourse until you have properly healed. We had to put a few stitches in around the sternum area, these will eventually dissolve. Bathe twice a day with cotton wool and warm water with TCP and use this special rectal rinse I shall prescribe. You can pick it up at the outpatient's pharmacy before you leave. Ill also give you a course of antibiotics in case there is any infection. Thank you, doctor, said Gordon.

Ben went to try and locate the car while Gordon tried to balance outside the Victorian entrance on crutches. When Ben pulled up, he leaned over and opened the door, come on hurry up I'm on double yellow lines. Gordon struggled and winced in pain as he got himself into the passenger seat. When they got back to the crescent Ben said, now get out and don't make a bloody fuss, don't look up and go straight inside. You've embarrassed me enough for one weekend.

Alistair and Renaldo watched out of their side window, Renaldo said I don't think you need crutches if you've had heart failure eh? Karl standing at the kitchen sink watched Gordon hobbling into number 5 and thought what's happened there I wonder.

Kris eventually made it downstairs about 3pm groaning. Karl was laying on a sofa still in his dressing gown and rabbit slippers working his way through a tub of Quality Street chocolates left over from Christmas.

The fucking state of you dear honestly said Karl. I know I'm sorry said Kris, Jesus I feel like shite. I bet you do, mind you I don't feel that great either. What's that in your riah dear? Kris put his hand up to his hair and stuck at the top was a bit of privet hedge. He pulled it out. Where did that bloody come from said Karl, did you creep down the bushes last night dear looking for a bit of trade? No, I did not said Kris. But then a flashback of the night before started to awaken in his fuddled brain. He pulled a cushion up to his face and groaned. What is it dear said Karl are you telling me porkies, ave you been out on the hunt for a bit of dick dear? No, I bleeding well haven't said Kris, it was them at number 5, Ben and Gordon, what? Do tell said Karl. I was just tidying up a bit, Karl scoffed, Kris continued, when I looked out of the window and I saw an ambulance flashing, so I pulled on me coat and went to have a look to see if I could help, Karl scoffed again, in Dorothy's feather cape? What? No! Oh well I don't know I can't remember; really do you want me to tell you or not? Said Kris. Yes, do go on dear I'm all ears said Karl. Well they brought that Gordon out on a stretcher, it must have been urgent as in the rush one of the ambulance men knocked me flying and I fell into a bush, hence the privet. Karl started laughing hysterically. Oh, gawd I can just imagine you in your feather cape and knickers staggering up the road, did anyone see you? Kris said quietly. They were all out of fucking course, gawping, said Kris. Oh, dear never mind said Karl, when you go out rise above it. I'll make us some breakfast.10 minutes later he placed a bacon and egg sandwich in front of Kris and a cup of coffee. Now I'm gonna sit here and watch you till you've bleeding well eaten the lot, right? Yes, said Kris, he could chuck it up later when he went up to shower.

Down at the Fawcett Inn Frank, Josh and Mary were getting the bar ready for the day's session. They were filling Mary in on the Tina Tits saga from the night before, Mary was laughing but saying ooo the pair of dirty conts, I 'ope yer gonna bar em. No, no need for that said Frank. Tina spends a fortune in here, and Larry's ok really said Josh. Luckily, we didn't lock them in all night, no harm done. They then went on to tell her about the drama up at the Crescent the night before. Frank had slept right through it, but Josh had been awake and up at the window watching. He described Kristabelle staggering up the street in feather cape and stiletto heels and falling in the bush. Mary was doubled up laughing, ooh fuckin ell I can't wait to see who comes in with the whole story later on. Josh went over to the front door and pinned it back for a bit to give the place a blast of fresh air. Mary said I'll go and check on the lunch prep in the kitchen.

Fat Gemma was in the kitchen getting the lunch ready. An 18 stone transvestite Gemma didn't look his best in the morning and struggled to get around the small catering kitchen situated behind the bar. Morning Gemma said Mary are you alright luv? Hi Mary said Gemma you alright girl? Yes luv, you look a bit fuckin knackered though did you ave a late night luv? What's happened to yer eyebrows said Mary gasping. Oh, I had a punter last night dear, got a thing about Divine, you know the dead singer, well I had to shave them off to look realistic. He pays a lot of money dear. I hope he bloody well does said Mary you look like a right cont now luv. Thanks, said Gemma. 'Ave you looked in the fooking mirror this morning luv said Mary. Yes, I know I look a sight but there you go I have to pay the rent love; I can't exist on what Frank and Josh pay me much as I love them to bits. Yes, well go and tidy yerself up a bit before service starts otherwise, you'll frighten the fooking customers to death when you bring the food out. Gemma carried on chopping away, He was trying to get some of the veg prep done for Sunday lunches tomorrow which were always busy at the Fawcett Inn.

They didn't serve dinner but had a good reputation for lunchtime food. In fact, on Sundays they had to have extra help in the kitchen and the bar.

The first customer through the door was a very shame faced Tina Tits armed with a bunch of flowers and a box of chocolates. You've got a fooking nerve said Mary. Ill deal with this said Josh. Well Tina? Said Josh, I'm so sorry said a beetroot red Tina. I'm so ashamed, so you should be said Josh. I'm not having that sort of thing going on in here Tina. It's a pub not a brothel. I know I'm sorry please forgive me it won't happen again. It had better not said Frank wagging his finger. I won't stop said Tina I feel like shit as you can imagine. I've got to pop round to Harry Harrington's Hotel in a minute and help him clean the rooms at the hotel, we've got a busy weekend this week. Alright see you later or tomorrow said Josh. Bye said an admonished Tina.

As he made his way down St James street en route to Harrington's hotel where he helped out when they were busy for a bit of cash in hand, Tina breathed a sigh of relief. He didn't know how he would have coped if they had of barred him. Living alone for 15 years now since his partner David had died, it was his only source except for helping Harry of communication. Harry came running down the stairs to let Tina in. Morning love said Harry, get your pinny on dear we have a lot of rooms to do this morning, I've got a couple in room 11 must have got up to all sorts last night dear by the state of the sheets. Tina felt himself retching, oh god how was he going to get through today. He followed Harry upstairs and grabbed a pile of fresh linen that Mavis, Harry's elderly mother had spent hours ironing. Harry was in his late 50's himself, single he and his mother ran this quite stylish hotel on their own, it was bang in the centre of Brighton with beautiful views of the splendid Indian style regency palace. They both worked hard but Harry was not great at the business side of things and instead preferred slipping over to the boutiques in the lanes and spending the electricity money on new clothes. Mavis had to chip in often with her pension to pay the bills. But she didn't mind, her little boy could do no wrong. Harry always a smart dresser, had unfortunately lost all of his hair. He would alternate between going bald or wearing an elaborately coiffured wig. He was a good natured sort who laughed very loudly at his own jokes, preferred alcohol to food and got his sexual kicks by servicing workman and commuters in one of the towns last gents' cottages (toilets) open, near Brighton station. He would make a day out of this on quiet hotel days and take a flask of coffee a bottle of brandy and some neatly cut sandwiches with him. He was high camp and could be very entertaining.

After they had finished the rooms Tina and Harry retired to the bar where Harry poured them both a large brandy to go with their coffees. Mavis went upstairs to have a lie down. Tina had Harry in hysterics explaining the drama of the evening before. I could have died with embarrassment when Frank walked in said Tina. I bet said Harry it's a wonder you never choked to death before sucking that Larry's dick you lucky cow. Ooh I know its enormous said Tina. Oh well I'd better go said Tina downing the Brandy, I'll just nip around to Morrisons to get my shopping and then I'll think I'll go back to bed I feel like shit. Ok love said Harry see you in the morning then, early mind they'll all be checking out, so I'll

54

need you to do all the rooms with Mavis after she has cooked breakfast. Ok are we still going to see Daisy Froglette tomorrow at the Fawcett Inn? Yes, bring your drag round here and you can shower in one of the rooms and well go around together. Ok love bye for now said Tina.

Back at the pub a nice crowd had started to gather. Weekenders mostly down from London. Saturday was like this in Brighton once the weather had started to pick up. Londoners headed for the coast. Gemma was run off of his feet in the kitchen, sandwiches, pizzas, and salads were flying out of the door. Larry came in and walked sheepishly up to the bar, sorry Frank about last night, am I barred. No, you're not this time, but take it as a warning I don't want that going on here ok. Tinas already been in with flowers and chocolates said Josh. Can I buy you all a drink said Frank eye ya can said Mary, you weren't even here said Frank indignantly! Doesn't fooking matter I was here in spirit. I'll have a glass of white wine for later. Frank got his wallet out. Tina, he thought of all people! He must try and find a boyfriend.

Most of the Crescent stayed in Saturday night the bars didn't do much in the way of entertainment as they were busy anyway. Some were a bit hungover from the night before. Alistair and Renaldo went out early doors for some tapas in the lanes (a very old part of the town consisting of winding little streets full of restaurants and little boutique shops) and went home to watch a film on Amazon Prime. John and Grant had Johns kids for the weekend, so they were definitely not going out to the bars anyway, opting for a few hours on the Pier and then a family meal at Donatello's restaurant in the lanes.

Cecil said to Mike do you want to go out for a couple of pints? Na said Mike Saturday night, there's bound to be loads of bloody hen do's going on, we had enough of all that in Blackpool. No save yourself for tomorrow.

Sunday was the big social day in Brighton. It had been like that for years. All the bars staggered the times and offered entertainment in some form. Mainly drag acts, but singers and live music too. It started at Hero's at 3pm the luxurious gay hotel on the seafront and worked its way around the gay village until closing time. The big draw of the week and you had to get in early to gain a space was Daisy Froglette's Sunday school party at the Fawcett Inn at 5pm. This ran along the lines of a Britain's got talent format. But called Brighton's got talent. Various acts would have their name down to do a spot. Daisy would sit on a big gold throne, if the acts met with approval she would pick up her extended long butterfly net and place it over the acts head or heads of the people and anoint them, they could go into the final round of the day. If the acts were terrible not only did, they get a pasting from Daisy's acerbic tongue, she would pick up her other tool, an extending hand with a pointed finger and poke them in the buttocks until they fell off the stage. With the audience jeering Off!. It was quite cruel in a Romanesque gladiator sort of way, but it was harmless, and everyone took it in the spirit it was intended.

The bar was rammed to the gunnel's as usual. Sunday roasts had been served and Gemma was busy loading the dishwasher in the kitchen helped by his landlady Wendy. Wendy had worked in a packing factory on in an industrial site in Moulscoombe a rundown suburb of Brighton where she and Gemma lived. So was known to all as "wrap it up Wendy" She was a bit rough, a chav really but had a heart of gold, she was grateful for any extra cash since the factory had closed. Olly was running around wiping the tables off and clearing any mess up so that the other punters could get a seat too if they wanted and Will had been roped in too, to help behind the bar.

There were 10 acts down for that session, the eventual winner the runner up and third place would go into the final for a £1000 prize on July 7th with the runner up getting £500. Third £250. The money was raised by donations in the buckets sent around the audience at each session, a weekly raffle for various local services donated by the local gay business community and topped up by Josh and Frank if necessary.

Tina and Harry Harrington had finished all the rooms, showered, and changed into their Sunday best outfits. they were sitting at the bar just polishing off their second very large Bloody Mary's. Pulling on their coats as it was still chilly outside but not raining thank god. Harry picked up one of Mavis broaches she'd left lying around and pinned it to the collar of his coat. You can't wear that! said Tina, who can't fuck 'em! Said Harry. So off they trolled around the corner making their way to get a front table at the Fawcett Inn before it got too busy. They were lucky and bagged one near the front next to Cecil and Michael.

This week there was a variety of acts from Brighton and the surrounding areas. They were mainly singers usually, but this week there were two strippers and a new boy band. Daisy Froglette had arrived made up to go on as the stairs were too much for her, she was sitting in the small area behind the stage to go on. Allana Cardinal in his carer, dresser role was just tweaking her wig and adding a layer of powder to the still handsome face. Frank took to the stage and introduced Daisy who came on to thunderous applause and whistling, took to her gold throne and sang her opening number. "There's no business like show business". She then started her usual patter and started reading out the names of the acts due to appear, taking the mickey where and when she could out of anyone in the audience she recognised.

The first act to appear was a young singer called Jonny Reynolds 19 and handsome. His backing track belting out Adele's "Rolling in the deep". He was really good, hit all the notes and moved around the stage with a sexy wiggle. Sitting in the audience John and Grant nudged each other and wondered if he needed a day job. The applause was great, and Daisy crowned him with the butterfly net and said young man you have done very well, your next test is the casting couch with me later on, if you pass that you'll be through to the final. The audience laughed and Jonny laughed, but looked a bit worried.

The next act up was another singer, an old face in Brighton who couldn't wait to get up and murder a ballad. Pushing 75 Terry Jones took to the stage with a mixture of cheers and boos. After he had warbled and slaughtered his way through "My Way" Daisy picked up the extended arm with the finger and rammed it into Terry Jones's buttocks while the audience yelled OFF. Terry unperturbed stuck his fingers up to the audience and went up to the bar to claim his free drink for taking part. What did this lot know, fucking wankers he thought to himself.

Then with much excitement from the audience. Daisy introduced the first Stripper. Adam Assmaster was 24 from Peacehaven, a builder by trade he was as fit as a butcher's dog, tattooed and muscular and when he jumped through the curtain there was an audible gasp from the audience. He did all the usual dance moves then jumped down into the audience and grabbed Tina's head and rubbed his jock strapped groin into his face. Oh God not her said Josh looking up from behind the bar. He then grabbed Harry' Harington's hand and pulled him up on to the stage and laid him on the floor while he pretended to fuck his face. Harry thought he'd died and gone to heaven until he went to get up. Unfortunately, he had got a bit too close to Daisy who managed to tread on Harry's wig near the top and kept her foot in place until Harry shot up hairless. The Audience were in hysterics, but Harry was furious. At the end when Adam Assmaster pulled off the jockstrap there was an audible gasp again as Adam revealed what they had all been waiting for, 10 inches of uncut pleasure. Adam took numerous bows, Daisy crowned him and anointed him with the butterfly net. Then winking at the audience said to Adam, what did you say your name was young man Adam Plasterer? No Assmaster said Adam, what dear I can't hear you can you come a bit nearer I'm going deaf in my old age too. Adam leaning over shouted in Daisy's ear ASSMASTER. With that Daisy's hand shot up and grabbed Adams Crown jewels and leaning forward, planted a kiss on his semi erect knob. You bastard said Adam laughing. Daisy cackled away and the audience were crying with laughter. Daisy called for a short refreshment

59

interval, yelling I need to lay down for a minute, I haven't had that much excitement my lovers since the old king died. When he was on a roll his original Dorset Burr came through with a vengeance.

During the interval Yo and Roz and two friends of theirs Caz and Jo took to the pool table for a friendly shoot. Caz and Jo were fairly new to Brighton. They had moved down two years before after selling their Islington pile for a king's ransom. Caz was a social worker and had got a job at Brighton council easily and Jo worked for the news team at the BBC and often worked from home. Occasionally she had to pop up to London and worst of all worlds twice a year had to attend seminars in the new BBC buildings up north in Salford. They had met Yo at one of the regular "Raise your skirt for diversity" workshops run by Brighton and Hove council. This was a feminist protest group that once a month met to as they put it "reclaim their cunts" The women all stood in a big circle having removed their knickers then raised their skirts to expose their vaginas. They would then stamp up and down angrily focusing on who they wanted to direct their hate at, usually Donald Trump or Harvey Weinstein. They would sway from side to side moaning and shouting, chanting in tongues, spitting out the name of that months hate figure. The object being to celebrate the diversity of their vaginas and by exposing themselves they were using their vaginas to scream at their oppressors. It was very cathartic. Even Roz thought she might like to go to that one!

But today they were all chilled and enjoying a game of pool, however Caz said to Yolanda I don't really feel comfortable in here Yo. I'm never sure whether I should be celebrating drag as a form of diversity or hating it because of the way it portrays women. I know what you mean said Yo, but I know most of them, they don't hate women it's just tradition like pantomime dame. However, when Daisy after the break bought on the second stripper of the day, they all downed their drinks and made for the door. Two penises in one day was too much to take even for the most liberal of lesbians.

The next stripper was Troy from Brighton. Not the best looker but a reasonable body. the crowd gave him a fair go but when he bent over in his white budgie smugglers revealing a nasty skid mark, there were cries of OFF OFF. Daisy not having noticed the nasty stain from where he was sitting, let him carry on. As he whipped his costume off holding it in his left hand at the end to reveal a very average small penis the crowd booed and heckled. Undaunted he bent over to take a bow and this time Daisy saw what the crowd were booing at. Disgusted he reached down and picked up his extending finger and rammed it into Troy's buttocks with such force he fell off the stage into the audience. Once they calmed down Daisy still holding the extending finger walked over to Tina's table and shoved the finger into Tina's drink, saying I shall need something that fucking strong to sterilize it. The crowd roared.

After the next average singer, the last act was the new boy band.

Jack 18, Harry 19 and Sam also 19. Three fit Lads from Hove and known as Bandit Boyz. They had been rehearsing for weeks in Jacks parents' garage. They did a mixture of cool vocal harmony, Rap and dance. Jack was the cute one. Harry the chav type all muscle and attitude and Sam was the pretty one. Together they were quite something. The Fawcett Inn crowd went crazy, Daisy whipped out a fan from her handbag and fanned her hot face. You could feel the excitement in the air, this act were dynamite. Daisy got off of the throne and made her way across to the lads to give them a good look close up. Cheers and Bravos went up as she anointed each one with the butterfly net. I'm sure we will be seeing plenty more of these three wont we. Yes, yelled the customers. Who had started yelling OFF OFF this time they meant get em off not get off. The lads made their way over to the bar where there was a soon a crowd around them offering to buy them drinks. Josh leant over the bar and said to Harry me and Frank come off duty in half an hour for a break, come with us for a drink around to the Queens Head we've got a proposition for you. Ok said Harry see you later with a wink.

The pub emptied out a bit after the show as the customers made their way to the next cabaret in Brighton or out to get some food.

Frank and Josh went over to the Bandit Boyz table and said are you ready. Sure, said Harry. The Five of them made it out of the door not unnoticed by those who were left. They walked down to the Queens Head which was relativity quiet until it was their turn to host the cabaret. In an hours' time it would be heaving so Josh said no beating about the bush have you lot got a manager yet?

No, we haven't got that far said Sam. Well you are going to need one soon said Frank. Josh here has many years' experience in Showbiz. He used to be a singer on the cruise ships. Really said Sam did you know Jane McDonald? Yes, laughed Josh she's a good mate of mine. I worked on several ships with her when I was just starting out, she's a lovely girl and a right laugh. Cool said Sam my Nan loves her. So, said Frank, Josh and I would like to manage you. I know all about contracts and booking agents said Josh and Frank can advise on security. He was in the army. What would be in it for you then said Jack? 20% of future earnings for the length of the contract plus the costs of promoting you. Ill handle your finances and make sure no one rips you off, don't expect to be millionaires overnight you'll have to work very hard for a while. We would want you to sign up for 5 years minimum at first. It's an expensive game launching acts like you, There's photo shoots, clothes, demo recordings. Phew said Jack do you think we were really that good? Yes, said Josh I watched the punters faces, you've got a youthful sex appeal sure, but you've got good voices too. Not that that's a problem said Frank look at some of the crap acts Simon Cowell has launched and they all laughed. Olly Murs ain't bad said Sam, fat arse though said Harry.

Look think about it said Frank. Go home and speak to your families, I take it you are all over 18 said Josh? Yes, said Harry I'm the eldest, 20 next week. We've all been mates for ages; our parents are all friends too. Well great think about it and let us know. We are going to grab a bite to eat, do you lads want to join us for a pizza. Love to said Harry the others nodded so they all made their way around to La Campannina the best family Italian restaurant in the city.

Monday morning arrived as it does in most households with groans, Ben got up and looked out of the window, it was raining. Never mind he'd cycle up to the train station instead of walking. He turned back to Gordon, I've rung into your work and left a message on the answer phone. I told them you had flu and a temperature. Thanks, said Gordon. Ben had been quite nice to him since he had come home. Even brought him up a cup of his favourite Earl Grey tea in bed. Now stay in bed today and try and rest said Ben I will said Gordon have a good day darling. Ok see you tonight said Ben leaning down and kissing Gordon full on the lips.

He ran down the stairs grabbing his coat and cycled furiously up to Brighton station. Parking his bike, he ran onto the platform only to hear an announcement that due to unforeseen conditions his train had been cancelled. Fuck it he said under his breath. The sixth time in two weeks. He managed to get into his office in Lambeth at 11am.

John and Grant were getting on nicely at the MP's house in Hove. Paul Bryan was there today not having to go up to London. He was getting on their nerves, to be honest he was giving them the creeps, every time they looked around, there he was leering at them. I've decided to knock through the whole of the downstairs and make it into an open plan living dining room and I want bi folding doors out onto the garden, but I need you to build an extension so that it will work properly. Well you will need to apply for planning permission probably for that bit said John. Don't worry I'll sort all that out with the planning officer. I don't care what it costs within reason but make sure I get receipts for everything please. How many more days will you be on the roof? We should have it finished by Friday said Grant. Ok I'm going back inside to do some office work give me a shout later when you are going. Ok I'll text you said John, last time he'd called up the stairs to say goodbye he'd got no reply so going up he knocked on the bedroom door, Paul had said come in, John nearly puked when he saw Paul laying on the bed watching porn wearing fish net stockings. He'd covered himself with a pillow, but he'd obviously been masturbating. Oh, sorry mate said John, no its alright said Paul come and join me if you like, err no you're alright thanks we are just off said John slamming the door and running down the stairs. They could hear peals of laughter coming from the bedroom window as they got into their van. Close shave said Grant laughing. Definitely said John, fucking creep I'll be glad when this jobs over.

Roz had her feet up on the coffee table and she was playing a video game. Lesbian gladiators. She had a big mug of coffee and a pile of hot buttered toast. She loved this "me time" She loved Yo but when Yo went off to work she relished this time alone to be herself. The doorbell rang and there was a delivery van from Vegan lifestyles outside. 2 Yurts for Yolanda Drinkwater said the fit looking guy with dreads. Blimey that was quick thought Roz, two are you sure? should only be one said Roz. 'No definitely two said the driver sign here please. Where do you want them said the driver? Better put them around the back said Roz. You'll have to help me they way a ton said the dreadlocked one. For Fucks sake said Roz it's me day off! Don't blame me I'm only delivering, come on then said Roz fuming.

Yolanda was in the staff room at the local primary school Queens Lane Infants. She was trying to whip up some enthusiasm for a climate change demo she was going to in London. Several of the other teachers were already going but there were one or two stick in the muds that tried to ignore her. Tanya Goodman the English teacher was digging in her heels. It alright for you Yo! you haven't got kids; I've got to see to mine after school. Yo thought I bet she's a closet Tory, she suspected a few of them were but they would never dare to admit it. She gave up for now, addressing Ms Wright (the diversity and sociology teacher) she said Jane, did you remember to print off those climate change charts and those pictures of all the fish dying in the sea and the penguins I sent you, Yes said Jane Wright I think the one with the penguin chick standing on that bit of ice on his own looking for his mother should get their attention. Bloody hope so said Yo, we had nothing like this at school when I was five years old. I knew nothing about climate change or sexual identity until I was at least 12, scandalous the education back then. We spent hours running around the playground playing sexist games like kiss chase and knew nothing about real life. It's called being a child said Tanya. Even children need to know they won't see 10 years old unless we change our ways said Jane Wright.

Alistair was putting together a tasty casserole made with pork fillet and roasted red peppers he was singing away to Doris Days greatest hits on the Cd player. He would get all his jobs done this morning as there was a nice film on this afternoon on talking pictures. Wuthering heights one of his favourites. He thanked god every day for his happy life.

Renaldo was at college teaching his class of 20 Spanish language students English. He enjoyed his job, but he was getting a bit stale, he needed a change.

He gazed out of the window. The grey sky again! Oh, he missed the blue skies of his homeland and the smell of the orange blossom. He loved England especially the springtime but every now and then he got a wrenching in his gut of home sickness. Pull yourself together he told himself and busied himself with some marking while the students watched a you tube presentation on pronunciation and dialects.

Karl and Kris were having a busy day in their summer house doing repair work on some of their costumes. After lunch they were going to start the cut outs for their summer ball out fits. They planned several costume changes for the big day. Tonight, we will get a big pad out and make lists of who to contact to get the marquee for the ball plus all the other things we will need, caterers etc said Kris. Yes, proper bleeding food this year said Karl, none of that mung bean crap that makes you fart all night. Oooo no none of that dear said Kris, elegant canapés is all that's required and plenty of booze. Yes, well Josh and Frank can see to that side of things said Karl. If they are not too busy with the bum boy band that was on at the pub yesterday. What are you on about said Kris, yes, they've got a boy band signed up, went down a storm yesterday at the talent show. Cecil texted me this morning. They took them out for a drink or something after the show. Said they were three beauties. Lucky Frank and Josh said Kris mind you they are not the type to play around its probably just business dear. My arse said Karl, it's the quiet ones what are the worst dear.

Frank was down in the cellar; Monday was his day for cleaning the pipes. Frank prided himself on his beer. Everything was stored in the correct date order.

His real ales were tapped and ready to stand for the correct time to clear before connecting up and his bottles and empty barrels were all neatly stacked for the draymen to collect tomorrow morning.

Mary was in the Kitchen having a cup of coffee while fat Gemma got on preparing that day's lunch. What's your specials today said Mary, pen poised ready to take down that day's menu. You'll be pleased said Gemma, I've made a big tray of Lancashire hot pot and I've had some salt beef cooking over night for hot salt beef sandwiches. OOO bloody luverly said Mary. Save us a bit of 'ot pot for me tea will ya luv? Sure, said Gemma. I'll make you a salt beef sandwich for your lunch too. Oh, tar darlin I'll put it in me 'andbag and 'ave a pic at it through the day. You know me luv, I'm only a picker, and if you've got any prawns going spare luv, I'll ave a few of those too. Do you ever do a food shop said Gemma? Not often luv, its only me init. Good job I feed you then isn't it said Gemma. Yes, it is luv, you may be a bit of a fat cont, luv but you've got a big heart too. Thanks, said Gemma I think and they both laughed.

Josh was upstairs in the little office next to Marys quarters. He was on the phone to his lawyer asking him to draw up contracts for the Bandit boyz. Make them watertight Solly, I don't want to be dumped if they hit the big time. I've a feeling these boys are going to be a hit.

Mary was holding court behind the bar. She had a regular following of her own, she called it her Monday club. Mainly older guys, some retired others well off and had retired early, a few of the professional dole merchants which Brighton tended to have more than its fair share of, and only one woman, Dolly, a lovely lady, an ex-licensee that used to have a pub in the lanes. Old school, Dolly always was dressed to impressed, hair done, nails painted, designer frock, diamond rings, immaculate. She still enjoyed a smoke and hated having to go outside to have one. "My god in my day darlings I must have breathed in 60 fags a day without lighting up, just from the fumes coming at me from the other side of the bar, never did me any harm. Because of that she had a gin soaked, husky deep voice like Fenella Fielding the 1960's actress from the carry on films. Everyone was fond of Dolly and she got bought a lot of gins on the Monday club session.

Mary had a lap top open on the bar and was scrolling through last minute.com to see if she could get a cheap holiday away somewhere straight after Easter. The pub went quiet then and it was a good chance to get away for a week. Reaching into her handbag she pulled out a bag of prawn's fat Gemma had given her. Anybody want a prawn she asked offering them round. I'll have a few said Dolly thank you Mary, Tina do you want one luv? No thanks dear I never touch fish. A few of the others mumbled rejections to. What about a bit of Salt beef? I've still got half of the one fat Gemma made me fresh at lunchtime. No, you're alright the others said. Suit yerselves said Mary. With that fat Gemma came out of the kitchen pulling on his coat said I'm off now Mary. All done in there are you luv, Yes Monday is never busy really is it, still we've taken a few quid and I've got some prep done for the week. Stay and have a drink with me before you go said Mary, I'm buying luv, ok ta said Gemma I'll have a pint of lager and lime I'm thirsty. Coming right up darlin' said Mary.

After giving Gemma his pint Mary went back to her holiday hunt while the others chatted away amongst themselves. After about 10 minutes she yelled out Bingo! It made some of the others jump. What? said pissy Michael one of her regulars what have you found? A week half board at the Helios hotel in Benidorm. It's a fucking bargain. £350 all in, plus flight of course. That's cheap said Dolly, what sort of hotel is it a bloody hostel? No, the Helios is dead posh dear, 4 stars modern, lovely it is. It's in the new town near all the bars. Anyone else want to come. Yeah put me down said Tina tits. Ok luv said Mary anyone else. I'll come said pissy Michael. Well I don't mind you coming luv said Mary but I'm not sitting next to you ont plane luv. Why not? said Michael affronted. Because last time you bloody well pissed yerself in the seat next to me and I could smell it all the way to Tenerife said Mary. I did not said Michael getting indignant. Yes, you did dear. Why do you think they call you pissy Michael in the first place? Because I drink too much said Michael, well it's not said Mary it's because you always stink of piss luv, you can't 'elp it I know its yer age dear, but I'll take you down to boots after this session and get you some of those incontinence pads for men. Ok said Michael embarrassedly thanks Mary. That's ok luv but your still not fucking sitting next to me ont plane though dear alright?

I've just texted Harry Harrington said Tina, he said can he come? says he'll be quiet at the hotel too. Yes, he can come said Mary I like Harry, I know he can be a bit of a cont when he's drunk like, but he's funny, always laughs at his own jokes though that one. Any more want to come? I'd love to said fat Gemma, but I could never afford it. I've never been abroad. Mary said when was the last time you had a holiday luv? When I was 9 years old said Gemma a week in Clacton with me gran, 20 years ago. That's terrible said Mary, pulling fat Gemma to one side she said quietly, what about if I lend you the money and you pay me back £20 a week? Oh, Mary would you do that for me really? said Gemma welling up. Course I would luv your good to me too. Thanks, said Gemma leaning down to give Mary a kiss on the cheek.

Fat Gemma's coming too said Mary, he's sharing with me aren't you dear? Am I? oh er yes said Gemma. I'll teach you how to put your fucking make up on properly dear so you might pull a bloke while your there. Fat chance of that said Gemma, oh you'll be alright over there in Benidorm. Some of those piss head lads down from Manchester will fuck owt dear, thanks said Gemma Laughing.

Right Michael, is there anyone you can get to share with you then dear keep the cost down? Said Mary. Not that I can think of said Michael despondently. What are you on about said Larry Allcock having just come into the pub.? We are booking to go to Benidorm said Mary we need someone to share with Michael. What pissy Michael said Larry? I'll pay for your flight Larry if you'll share with me said Michael. Larry paused for a bit, Michael had a few bob it could work out well, then said oh go on then why not, I can scrape the rest together, mind you if you piss yerself Mike I'm not cleaning up after you. Don't worry said Mary I'm taking 'im down to boots later to get 'im sorted out.

Right that's great said Mary, hand your cards over dears and I'll book the holiday for us all. Don't you want to come Dolly said Tina tits, no thanks dear said

Dolly I'm going to my sister's villa in Marbella soon. What about Josh and Frank said Gemma they won't want us both away at the same time will they? said Gemma, leave them to me said Mary. Start getting your mate wrap it up Wendy boned up in the kitchen. I suppose I could prepare a lot and leave it in the freezer said Gemma. That's the ticket said Mary we'll sort it out. Let's all have a drink to celebrate. They were all starting to get into the holiday mood. Dolly after her fifth large gin slurred, I wish I was coming too now. Well why don't you said Mary your welcome. I just don't like sharing that's all said Dolly. Well book a room on your own said Mary. Dolly paused see if they've got a proper suite Mary if they have, I'll come. They've got a VIP section on the top floor I do know that; I've stayed there before. Ok see if its available. It was, so Dolly said fuck it dear book it!

When Josh and Frank popped into the bar to say cheerio before they headed out for the rest of the day as Monday was their night off, there was quite a party going on in the bar. Someone had streamed Viva Espana by Sylvia to the pub sound system and Tina and Dolly were up on the stage flamenco dancing with some castanets Mary had found behind the bar. Seems very lively said Josh everything alright Mary. Oh yes just a bit of high spirits I'll keep me eye on it. Go on you two bugger off and have a night out somewhere you need a rest. Ok darling they both bent down and kissed her on the cheek and shouted goodbye to the others as they left the pub.

Josh and Frank made their way home, they were going to have a little siesta and then get showered and go out somewhere for a meal. Monday nights they usually took a drive out somewhere into the country and treat themselves to a nice meal. One or two places opened on Monday, many of the restaurants choosing Tuesday to close for their rest day. Josh's mobile rang, it was Harry, Hi Harry what's up said Josh. Nothing much just a few questions, what are you doing? Going home for a rest said Josh, then we are going out for dinner. Lucky you I'm bored stiff said Harry, ah that's a shame, what are the others doing? Sam's out with his Mum tonight at bingo and Jack is getting his hair streaked and cut again laughed Harry. So, I'm home alone Billy no mates. Frank who had been listening on the car phone said, well if you don't mind being with us two old gits you can join us for dinner later if you like. Josh nudged Franks leg and scowled, what? mouthed Frank silently. Really guys do you mean it I'd love to said Harry. Ok well pick you up about 7.15pm said Frank. Wear something smart, I'll try said Harry who lived in his trackies and trainers.

What did you say that for said Josh? Oh well he's a nice kid he's on his own, you mean you fancy him said Josh, well don't you said Frank chuckling, Josh smiled a bit said Josh. We'll see what happens said Frank.

When they arrived to pick Harry up later that night, he came out of his house in Hove dressed nicely, tight designer ripped jeans a tight white shirt unbuttoned and very expensive trainers on. Frank whistled; you scrub up well don't you. Harry blushed and got in the car. Where are we off to then. A nice country pub out Cuckfield way then to dinner, hope it's not too expensive said Harry I've only got 50 quid? Don't worry we'll claim it off expenses said

Josh winking at Harry. Harry blushed again. He found both of them hot, he preferred older men, He was definitely into the sexy daddy types. When they dropped him home later, he leant forward from the back and gave them both a quick kiss on the lips each. Phew he is hot said Josh as Harry put his key in the door and turned around and waved goodnight,

Friday had arrived and soon it was the weekend again.

Gordon was now out of bed the swelling had gone down and he was more comfortable and looking forward to going out for a drink on Sunday afternoon.

Ben had been quite nice to him, but he hadn't seen too much of him as Ben had stayed in London for a couple of nights as he was in the middle of an important court case. His phone rang at that moment. It was Ben sounding very jubilant. He and his team had won their case in court and stopped the deportation of the drug dealer. Ben had got him off on a technicality, Ben's speciality. They had made their way from the courtroom straight to one of the trendy bars near Borough Market and were celebrating in style. The dealer's girlfriend was splashing the cash and Ben said I'm sorry I won't be home again tonight I'm gonna stay over at Jazz's pad, Jasmine was Ben's secretary. Sorry Gordon but we have just started celebrating and it's gonna be a heavy night. Ok congratulations said Gordon trying to keep the disappointment out of his voice. I'll be home tomorrow about 12pm said Ben giving the thumbs up to the dealers 23 year old cousin waiting with a big smile and a lunch box to match at the bar, bye for now. Bye said Gordon have fun. Ben made his way over to cousin Durak who was leaning against the counter in a sexy manner, his heart beating fast. Well he deserved a big bonus for getting uncle Florim off, didn't he? He had never tried Albanian cock before and was dying to try. Durak handed him a glass of champagne, thanks said Ben your velcome said Durak with an impossibly deep voice for a 23 year old. Bens pulse was racing.

Gordon opened the freezer door and helped himself to a handful of ice, He opened the drinks cupboard and selected a bottle of Absolute Vodka he poured himself a triple and topped it up with fever tree tonic. Sod it he thought, he picked up his mobile phone and rang his boss at Mission Accomplished. Hi Jan, It's Gordon. I'm much better thanks I'll be in in the morning ok? Fed up with sitting around the house he couldn't wait to get back to work.

Roz and Yolanda were busy in the garden trying to erect the Yurts. I thought I told you one Yo said Roz, I know hun said Yo, but you got 50% off if you bought a second one it was too good to resist. Roz sighed, lucky we've got a big garden, look we will get this one up today before I go to work, and I'll try and finish the other one on Sunday. Pray it doesn't rain. Yo threw her arms around Roz and kissed her, you are the best said Yo you really are. I know said Roz softening. Finish that one off then come upstairs said Yo. Roz smiled and picked up her mallet and started to hammer in a large peg with gusto.

Michael and Cecil had just finished off their fish supper and were clearing up after their tea. Let's hope one of us has better luck tonight said Cecil. Eye we could do with a few extra quid to spend in Benidorm said Mike I can't wait to get away. Well only two more weeks and we'll be there said Cecil. Sun Sangria and Sex. You can stick that bloody sangria said Mike. Cecil laughed I'll just go up and get changed and get me bingo bag and we can be off. Yes, don't take fookin hours I want to get there early and have a bevy first.

Yolanda stretched out and yawned and nudged Roz, you had better get up hun, I'll just go and get our dinner ready, Ok yawned Roz she could have stayed there all night, Yo had been particularity giving earlier. We've got spaghetti bolognaise tonight said Yo. Ok love I'll shower and come down. She didn't mind the Quorn mince it was a bit more like meat than some of the other shit she had to endure.

After dinner Yolanda said I'm just going to pop over to Kris and Karl's for a natter, I've got a school project I want to discuss with them. Ok said Roz I'll read the paper for a bit. What was Yo up to now she thought. Oh well turning to the sports pages she soon lost herself.

Yo rung on number seven's door. It was 7.30pm by now. Karl answered, Hello Yo what can we do for you. Do you mind if I come in for a minute, I've got a favour to ask you? Oh, ok we are just having our aperitifs can I get you something? No, you're ok thanks, hello Kris how are you? fine dear thank you come and sit down. What can we do for you? Well I was wondering if you would like to come to the school I teach at in Queens Lane, and do some story telling for the children as The Royal Sisters.

What come and do a drag act in the school? said Karl a bit surprised. Well no not a drag act more a story reading said Yo but dressed up in your female attire. I'm sorry Yo why would you want us to do that? said Kris. Its part off our diversity curriculum said Yo. We feel it's very important for children to accept that there are different genders and lifestyles, different sexualities, that they can learn from an early age that its ok to be different, many of them are born into the wrong bodies and feel trapped. You can see the confusion on their faces sometimes she sighed, so this way we can say look it doesn't matter who you are, what you wear or who you love it's OK! Yes, well very noble dear said Karl but what age are we talking about? Well approximately 5-11 year olds said Yo.

Aren't they a bit young said Karl? Oh no said Yo Ideally, we would have started this scheme several years ago, the younger the better. We won't stamp out homophobia and racism if we don't nip it in the bud at a young age. What about the parents? Said Karl? Well mainly they are all quite progressive around here, there are a few chavy, whoops sorry underprivileged types from the estate up near the racecourse that might object but to be honest they are the ones we need to reach out to the most.

Well if we agree what's in it for us are you asking us to do it for nothing? said Kris. No! No! not at all I wouldn't expect you to do it for nothing what do you think is appropriate? Well who's paying for It? said Karl. Oh, I've got a grant from Brighton and Hove council said Yo. £250 said Karl, cash, done said Yo. Kris looked at Karl in amazement. What shall we read them? said Karl, well something you think maybe appropriate, something children like said Yo. How about Snow white and the 7 dwarfs said Kris sarcastically, well yes that could work except we would have to call it Snow White and the seven little people, dwarf is an offensive term now. Karl scoffed, and of course Snow White was an oppressed female said Yo warming to her theme. We could make out that the charming prince who comes to kiss her really identifies as a woman and after a sex change he is now known as Sharon said Karl tongue firmly in cheek, Oh yes Yo exclaimed that's marvellous, clapping her hands together, although we do prefer the term gender realignment now, not sex change and maybe Sharon isn't really a gender neutral name, maybe we could call her Jamie? Like Jamie Curtis. Whatever floats your boat dear said Kris, we can do it as a little play if you like with a song at the end said Kris downing a large gin and tonic in one hit. Oh yes, I like that idea said Yo. So, when do you want us to do this? said Karl. Well we are breaking up for Easter soon so a week Thursday ok. Karl looked in the diary, yes that's ok what time? 2pm ok said Yo? Yep that's fine said Karl we'll get there about 12.30 to get set up. We will let them go home after for the Easter holidays, they'll all leave happy and enjoy their break. I'll get a letter out to the parents first thing Monday morning said Yo. Thanks guys I really appreciate it, I'll let myself out, bye for now. As she slammed the door the guys looked at each other and burst into laughter. £250 quid to read a bleeding fairy story said Kris I can't believe you asked that much. Oh well look at it as a council tax rebate dear we pay the fuckers enough. Plus, we've got some costumes out in the summer house that'll do nicely, we'll have a look tomorrow, you've got a Snow White and I've got an evil queen frock left over from when we did that adult panto thing for the prisoners at Wandsworth nick. Yes, I've still got the script somewhere said Kris. Well we can't use that dear it's for children after all said Karl. Well we can alter it a little bit they won't know what we are on about, anyway I fucking hate kids.

Saturday morning came and Fat Gemma was in the kitchen peeling a big sack of potatoes ready for tomorrows Sunday roast dinners with Wendy. He was running through the menu with her. I'll keep it simple for the week I'm away, basically I'll freeze loads of pies you can defrost, Ill roast a big piece of beef, some chickens and a loin of pork for the roasts. You can stick to pizzas salads and sandwiches for the week plus hot pot and pies sandwiches etc, that should do you it's always quiet that week after bank holiday. Does Josh and Frank know yet you're going away said Wendy? No, they don't said Gemma I'm waiting for Mary to square that one.

Mary was in the office just then with Josh and Frank explaining that she had asked Gemma to come on holiday with her to Benidorm.

Well have you booked it said Frank? Yes, luv it's all done I'm sorry I should have asked you first. It all happened a bit quick. Yes, you bloody well should have done said Josh. Why are we always the last to find out about what's going on around here? Well Gemma's been here a long time Josh he's reliable in the main and he's never had a break, never been on holiday since he was nine. Well that's not my fault said Josh. Plus he can share with me, I know he's really a man but he's more like a woman and it 'll make the room cheaper for me luv. So that's it laughed Frank. Well part of it laughed Mary but you know if I share with the others they may get pissed, drag back a bit of trade. I can't be doing with all that at my age. What if Gemma drags back a man said Josh. Oh fuck off who's gonna shag that now, come

79

on really you must be joking darlin' Oh the caring mother role you were just playing didn't last long did it said Josh. Mary laughed you'll be alright he's gonna show Wendy the ropes and your here if she needs a hand. Thanks, said Josh. Oh alright bugger off we'll manage but in future ask first ok? Ok I'm sorry said Mary.

She went downstairs stuck her head around the kitchen door. Its ok its sorted luv, start packing. Oh, great said Gemma I'll nip up to Primark after lunch and see if I can get a few bits, a new bikini maybe. No! no fookin bikini said Mary I'm not 'avin you make me look a right cont laying around the pool. T shirt and shorts will do.

Ben got home about 12'0clock, he was in a foul mood. Last night's party with Durak hadn't gone a bit as planned. Durak had taken him back to a Premier Inn hotel courtesy of Florim. Actually, Florim had paid for a deluxe room at the Hilton in Park lane but Durak had booked the Premier Inn near the London eye and pocketed the rest of the cash. On arrival Ben said there must be some mistake I can't stay in a Premier Inn! Why not said Durak they have a bed and a shower come on he said grabbing Ben's hand and pulling him through the door. It was really late about 2am now and they had both had a lot to drink and had done a fair bit of Charlie too as well. Where else you gonna go this time of night eh?

When they entered the room, Ben winced as he saw the furnishings, he started to get undressed as Durak poured them both a large scotch from a bottle in his overnight bag. Ben hung his jacket and shirt up tidily and looked around for the trouser press, there wasn't one, he should have known, he hung them on a separate hanger. After they had drunk the whiskey down in one, Durak stripped his own clothes off. Ben blanched at the size of Durak's cock. Durak pushed Ben on top of the bed, he was so strong he had been junior middle weight champion in Albania and pinned him down. His cock rock hard he forced himself into Bens mouth, pulling Bens head up to take his manhood down as far as it would go, Ben was choking and gagging but Durak took no notice. When he tired of this, he flipped Ben over and ripped down Bens silk boxers spat on his hand and rammed himself inside Ben. Ben yelled out in pain. Durak said shut your mouth bitch and shoved Bens boxers into his mouth, what did you think, you would be doing this to me eh pussy boy? Ben laid there in agony until Durak had finished and rolled off of him and fell asleep. He had just been raped.

He laid there as silent tears fell down his face. What should he do? He couldn't report it to the police the gang would have him killed. He couldn't use the law; his image would be ruined. He knew he could say nothing, he laid there for half an hour before creeping to the bathroom, he was bleeding quite badly, he got in the shower and rinsed himself off. He got dressed in silence trying hard not to yell in pain and gathered his things. Durak was passed out on the bed still naked and snoring. He crept out of the room and hailed a taxi in the street to take him to Jasmines flat in Clapham junction. He had a latch key and when he got there, he let himself in really quietly laid on the bed in the spare room and wept. He would get his revenge somehow.

He called out Gordon I'm home, no answer, He walked into the kitchen and saw a note on the table.

Gone to work as I feel much better, see you tonight. That bitch should have been here to greet me he thought, he had it coming thought Ben. He slowly made his way upstairs ran a hot bath with radox liquid and carefully got into the bath, He was so angry, plus he felt a bit stupid for letting himself get talked into accepting a night with Durak plus a parcel of cocaine as part payment for his fee. Afterwards he swallowed two paracetamol and climbed into bed.

Daisy Froglettes Sunday school produced a beautiful girl singer called Lauren Anderson, and a stand up drag comic called Sandy Lane, both were through to the finals.

Gordon never got to go out for his Sunday lunchtime fun as Ben was laid up in bed with some mystery illness and being a bastard yelling out all of his demands. Still Gordon quite liked that.

The bandit boyz had turned up to view the competition. Harry stayed on after the show, the other boyz went home. Jack to his hairdresser girlfriend and Sam home to mum. Harry went out with Frank and Josh for a meal later and ended up staying the night.

Monday morning when they all woke up in the same bed another horny session took place. Josh couldn't get over Harry's rough beauty, the chiselled face the tasteful tattoos, piercing blue eyes. Frank couldn't believe his luck he now had two of the most beautiful guys in Brighton in bed with him. He was well chuffed.

Frank said to Harry, we think you are great mate and we would like to do this again, sure anytime said Harry leaning over and kissing Frank and grabbing his still semi hard cock. But said Josh in our position we don't want any gossip. We don't sleep around, we have been very discreet on the odd occasion It's happened, so when we leave later, you'll have to get in the boot of the car until we leave the crescent. Oh, ashamed of me are you said Harry jokingly. No not at all said Josh your gorgeous but we must keep it to ourselves and especially the other two boys, otherwise there will be hell to pay, jealousy etc. Yeah you may be right said Harry. Ok daddies he joked I'm up for that, our secret. With that he pulled Josh towards him and gave him the most passionate kiss Josh could ever remember receiving.

Thursday morning

Kris and Karl were going over their lines for the fairy tale reading at the school later. They had roped in Yo for a bit part she was to play the transgender prince. We'll get some of the kids to come and sit on the stage with us for the 7 dwarfs, I mean little people said Karl. Do we 'ave to said Kris. Yes, don't be horrible said Karl I've found a box of caps and false noses and things they can wear. Can't wait said Kris.

Their costumes and make up box were ready by the door. All checked over Sunday morning, everything ironed, and all props laid out as the two professionals they were.

Yo was busy at the school. She was arranging chairs for the parents to come and watch the little end of term show. She was surprised and rather hurt because she had some angry phone calls and emails from some of the parents, demanding that the show be cancelled and that they were withdrawing their children for the last day of school. She was particularly hurt by the angry accusations she was getting from some of the Muslim parents who did not want their children taught about homosexuality or any other kind of sexuality. She had tried to say to one very vocal father, It's not about sex it's a fairy tale, just a modern version. But you have two men dressed up as women to tell the story! Said Mr Khan at the other end of the phone. Yes, because they are representing different gender identities. Lots of people are born in the wrong body or just identify as something different, we want to encourage children to be free and honest said Yo. Rubbish and it's against Allah's will said Mr Khan. We must all respect each other's cultures Mr Khan, we accept yours! I've been on dozens of save Palestine marches in my time, I regularly fast for Ramadan in solidarity with you people. I'm an active member of BLM (black lives matter) That's up to you said Mr Khan we didn't ask you to. In our community we practice and respect sharia law not your infidel laws. But you are in England, we are a multicultural society we must all accept everyone's differences and embrace them Mr Khan. How else are we going to enrich society if we don't reach out to all cultures, all genders, all people said an exasperated Yo. I'm warning you miss there will be repercussions if you go ahead with this shouted Mr Khan you will not do this to our children, and he slammed the phone down.

Stupid man thought Yo furious after the call. She said to Ms Wright here we are trying to oppose racism and intolerance and its men like that who are enforcing it onto themselves. I sometimes think they don't want to live in a multicultural society at all!

That afternoon Kris and Karl pulled up to the school and were amazed to see about 20 people waving placards and shouting no to homosexuals, no sex in schools, save our children. There was lots of yelling. Most of the protesters seemed to be from the Muslim community but there was a few irate looking Caucasians and a black couple too.

What the fucks going on said an alarmed Kris. Fuck knows I'll just drive through the gate said Karl. As they got nearer the gate the crowd turned and spotted the sisters approaching in their huge Volvo XC90. The fact they had a basic slap on and 4 pairs of theatrical eyelashes each had probably given the game away. Karl lowered the window a bit as a man approached, it was Mohammed Khan. You can't come in here he said we do not want perverts in here. Who the fuck are you said Karl? I'm representing the parent's group who are opposed to sex education for minors. I don't give a fuck who you are dear we are booked to work here today, and you won't stop us shouted Karl, Eyelashes going like the clappers in his anger. Just then a woman in full burqa and niqab banged on the window Kris's side and started yelling abuse in a language he didn't understand. Shove it up your fat arse Mary yelled Kris through the glass and gave the woman the finger while clutching his Snow White wig on its stand in his other hand. Just then a man and a woman wearing Christian aid T-shirts jumped onto the bonnet of the car. Fuck this said Karl. He yelled out of the window fucking move or I'll drive off. The crowd moved in closer trying to intimidate them. Several more women fully covered in their black veils started screaming at them. Right hold on said Karl. He clicked the gear stick into sports mode shoved his foot down on the accelerator and tore off towards the gate. The two Christian aid workers went flying landing on top of a burqa clad woman and a man with a long beard knocking them to the floor. The sisters sailed through the gates down the drive towards the school where Yo and the headmaster Jez Butler were waiting for them.

As Kris and Karl got out of the car Yo and Jez rushed forward. Oh, we are so sorry said Jez, are you ok said Yo? so sorry about the commotion. We don't understand it at all. Yes, we're alright said Karl inspecting the bonnet of the car. Don't worry said Kris we've had worse haven't we dear. Yes, dear we had a booking once at The Prince of Wales pub in Brixton one night during the riots. That was scary! said Kris but it didn't stop us, we just drove straight through the bastards. The show must go on said Karl. Thank you said Yo your so brave. Na said Karl it'll take more than a few bleeding walking letter boxes to stop me from working dear. Yo gasped but didn't say anything. Jez had gone bright red and was staring at his feet, shifting backwards and forwards on his sandals. Right take us to the little fu..... I mean little dears said Kris. This way said Jez.

Michael and Cecil were happily ensconced in the Weatherspoons bar at Gatwick Airport enjoying a few pints of Stella and a full English breakfast each, eagerly awaiting their easy jet flight to Alicante. I can't fooking wait said Mike. Nor me, I know we never rarely go anywhere else, but I still get that butterfly feeling in my stomach every time we go said Cecil. Eye I know what you mean said Mike I feel same. I'll text the Duchess in a minute to let him know we are arriving on time, thank god said Cecil. Tell him we should be at the hotel by 5pm said Mike.

Alistair and Renaldo were already installed happily in their hotel in Valencia. They had flown out the day before on the Wednesday. So, they could stay three nights and then drive down to Benidorm to meet Cecil and Mike on the Saturday afternoon. The first night they had enjoyed a quiet meal in the old quarter and today they were going to meet up with Renaldo's parents and two brothers and four sisters and their children at the grandmothers enormous apartment which was walking distance from the hotel for a family lunch Spanish style. Renaldo was very excited. I can't wait to see them all again, yes it will be lovely for you, and you too I hope said Renaldo. I'm sure it will said Alistair squeezing his shoulder. Trying to cram in all the museums and art galleries was going to be a push but they were determined to do the best they could with their time.

On arrival at grandmothers, the whole family made a big fuss, there was lots of kissing lots of noise and a 3 hour lunch with a plethora of traditional Valencian fayre, the centre piece of course being the Paella. Renaldo was a different person thought Alistair, very animated and did he dare to think it happy.

Michael and Cecil landed on time and caught the shuttle bus from outside of the airport to take them into Benidorm. When they arrived at the stop in Benidorm, they had to drag their cases all through the old town and up the hill to the Casa Don Philippe hotel as the roads were to narrow and busy to try and get a taxi. They didn't mind, the place was heaving and the atmosphere buzzy and exciting. Being Easter, the resort was packed with families from all over Spain and the locals. Easter was a very serious affair too, with lots of parades and music, some very solemn but also there was lots of gaiety as they turned off the walking street as the English called it and up a side road known to all as tapas alley, they knew they were back in Spain. Little bars and restaurants displaying windows full of tempting tapas and pintxos the little snacks on sticks that even Mike liked. There was an aroma of garlic and fish that was mouth-watering. At the top of the road they turned right and were opposite the campest little hotel in Benidorm. "The Duchess" Philippe was waiting by the door for them and greeted them with his usual bonhomie kisses and cuddles, hello my loves so lovely to see you again. Oh, its lovely to be back said Cecil we've missed you. Oh, that's nice I've missed you too. I bet your dying for a drink? You bet said Mike plonking himself down on a seat at the narrow bar. Angelo, he said to the barman two big vodka and tonics no ice please. How the fook do you remember that said Mike. It's my job luv said Phillipe. (Phillipe, Philip was from the north too) Your rooms are all ready and I'll get Angelo to take your bags up, now then my dears tell me all the gossip.

Back at Queens Lane preparations for the Snow White story telling were getting under way, although it was starting to represent a mini pantomime set now. Kris and Karl had taken over and were scooting around for props for the stage. They found two big back throne style chairs at the back of the stage and dressed them up with feather boas and placed them centre stage They found an old art easel and hung their own prop mirror on it, it had no glass in it just the frame. Yo started experimenting with the lighting and they got a soft pink light that wasn't too harsh They found some old scenery of trees and bushes and pulled that onto the stage within 45 minutes they had transformed it onto a little panto scene. Yo was amazed. Oh, you are so talented. We know said Karl. They did a quick sound test the microphones were working ok. Right said Kris show us to our dressing room. Er I'm sorry I didn't think about it said Yo. Well you don't expect me to stand up here in my drawers do you in front of the kids said Kris? No of course not I do apologise. Hang on let me think. Ah I've got it she said follow me they grabbed their bags and followed her down the corridor. You can use our new gender neutral toilet facility said Yo. Throwing back the door with pride, it was quite nice thought Karl a long mirror, nice over lighting plenty of sinks a few stools to sit on. This ok said Yo? Yes, its fine dear thanks said Karl. I'll leave you to settle in then boys break a leg. Ta said Kris. Not bad eh said Kris considering some of the shit holes we've had to change in over the years. First things first said Kris, he reached down into his bag and whipped out two large plastic glasses a bottle of gin and a few cans of Schweppes tonic he'd even remembered the ice and a few slices of lemon. Fuck me said Karl what are you like dear. Come on have one said Kris where going to need a few I think, well just a small one for me said Karl.

Yo was standing with Jez and Ms Wright and a few of the other teachers welcoming the parents that had come into the assembly hall. When all the mums and dads were settled, they let the children in from the playground who were all really excited, but they got them all into lines and sat down nicely in front of the parents. The parents all seemed good humoured. A mixed bunch, quite a few house husbands, professional couples, plenty of the grungy green types that lived in the area. A few mums with top knots and tracksuits sharing big bags of crisps. Yo was disappointed with the ethnicity of the group. Only one black couple and a few Filipino women. What's wrong with some people she sighed to herself.

The sisters were ready and made up in the wings. Kris was fortified and ready to get at 'em. Yo stood at the mic dressed as the prince charming in black leggings and a tight waistcoat welcomed everybody and said please put your hands together for the fantastic Royal Sisters. They hit the cd button as the lights lowered and the Disney theme from Snow White 'When you wish upon a star' echoed around the assembly hall. Kris came on in his Snow White outfit sweeping the stage with a broom and whistling like Snow White in the film. There was a big cry of ah from the children. Kris put down the broom and sat on one of the thrones and picked up a big book from the table beside him.

Hello boys and girls, nothing. I said Hello boys and girls. Hello Snow White shouted the children and parents. I'm going to read you a little story of what happened to me when I was out walking in the forrest but first let me introduce you to my friend the old queen of the forest. Karl fluttered on stage with a fairy wand and black curly Cher wig. Hello boys and girls, hello old queen yelled the children Karl turned and gave Kris daggers. Kris pretended not to notice, he said, and we need 7 little people to come up on stage with us to help us tell the story, who will it be? Me yelled the children lots of hands shooting up. Karl chose 7 he could see near the front.

Come on then up you come, and he said right your sleepy here's your cap and your grumpy he said to this little girl. I'm not grumpy she said I'm Kylie, yes you are dear now move along, I told you I'm not grumpy she said stamping her foot. Kris got up and said this way dear and grabbed her hand and yanked her away. That's it my little loves move along now all put your caps and noses on and we will continue with the story, come and sit around our feet and we will read to you said Karl.

It was all going ok until. The little people started giggling. Kris looked up from the book and said sorry, what are you laughing at my dears? Please Miss, Dozy just farted miss said Sleepy, it bloody stinks miss said Grumpy, Dozy said no I haven't miss and started making a rude sign at Grumpy putting his finger through a hole he'd made with the thumb and forefinger of his left hand. Look miss said Grumpy he's making the fucking sign. Now children calm down said Karl shocked at the language, listen closely if you want to get some sweeties at the end. He tried not to sound menacing, but it was hard.

When Karl got up and walked to the mirror to do the famous mirror on the wall who is the fairest of them all scene, a voice from one of the top knotted mothers yelled out not you fat slag.!All the children started laughing their heads off. Chanting fat slag, fat slag, fat slag.

Jez Butler the headmaster jumped up and shouted That's enough, quiet. Any more of that madam and I'll have to ask you to leave, now children settle down and don't spoil the story. Karl was absolutely livid. Kris who was half pissed got the giggles and couldn't carry on for a few moments.

Somehow they got to the end and just when Yo was leaning over to kiss Snow White to awaken her from the sleep, a loud noise came from the back as the doors flew open and in charged Mohammed Khan with the rest of the protesters and two police officers yelling there we are officer a lesbian sex show!

Nobody got arrested, the rest of the teachers got up and separated the crowd. Some of the mothers were trying to have a punch up with the burqa clad women, children were screaming, but Yo calmed then down chucking sweets at them while Jez with the police officer got the protesters out of the building. Kris and Karl stormed off stage and had a huge row in the gender neutral toilet, while Yo sat with her head in her hands in the assembly hall mortified and was being comforted by Ms Wright.

Once she pulled herself together, she and Ms Wright made their way to the gender neutral toilet to pay off the Royal Sisters. I'm so sorry guys she said to the sisters, Karl held his hand out, so you fucking should be, MONEY! Yo handed over the envelope with the £250 in it. It should have been £500 for what we've had to go through with these little brats and their awful bloody parents said Kris. We are sorry said Ms Wright would you like to come into our safe room and meditate for a bit, it will help us all to calm down. I can make us some chamomile tea. You can shove that shit right up your chutney box said Karl we're out of here, now MOVE! Ms Wright looked like someone had just been told her cat had died. The sisters made their way out of the front door, there was still a bit of commotion and Mohammed Khan was shouting through a loud speaker NO to homosexuals, Karl marched right up to him and knocked the speaker from his hand and headbutted him hard and said take that you intolerant cunt If you don't like our ways fuck off back to your own country. A big cheer went up from some of the parents still leaving.

GOOD FRIDAY

The bank holiday Easter weekend arrived. Some of the crescent stayed home to avoid the crush as the out of towners arrived. The Fawcett Inn was packed to the gunnels on the Friday night, it was all hands to the deck all over town, the weather was good for a change and the atmosphere was Party!

Saturday

At the Casa Don Phillipe Michael and Cecil were just having a coffee at the bar before walking down to Granny's tea rooms for a full English breakfast. The Casa didn't do food as it was a small boutique hotel and only offered continental style coffee and croissants. The guys were having this as their first course. Alistair and Renaldo were due to arrive about midday and they thought they would just have a wander around the shops until they arrived.

Alistair and Renaldo had packed up and then popped around to say goodbye to grandma who made them promise to come back soon. Te extrano Renaldo wept his Grandmother, I miss you too, all of you said Renaldo a big lump in his throat.

Renaldo was very quiet on the drive from Valencia and Alistair rightly guessed he was a bit upset about leaving his family. But, by the time they reached the beautiful area of Altea he had livened up and was talking excitedly about what they would get up to next. Another 10 Minutes and the big high rise blocks of Benidorm appeared in the distance, from afar they looked quite majestic, as they got closer Alistair's heart sank and he said oh dear I don't like the look of this. Don t worry said Renaldo, don't let it put you off, its actually great fun. They have to have so many hotels because it's so popular, it is still the number one destination for Spanish people to come on holiday. Really said Alistair, I thought it was all Brits on the piss. No not at all said Renaldo, one little section of it is a bit like that but it's a massive place and the rest of it is quite cool. Renaldo knowing Benidorm quite well knew it was going to be a nightmare to park. They drove around the old town a few times and eventually he found a spot down near the Parc de Elche, known to all as "Dove park" because there were always dozens of white doves in the area. Getting out of the car Alistair's heart lifted as he got a good look at the Poniente beach, oh I say that's beautiful said Alistair. Yes 3 km long and the sand is cleaned every night. There was a pretty harbour area to their left, lots of big palm trees and the sun was shining brightly. Follow me said Renaldo. They dragged their suitcases on wheels towards the town and Renaldo had great fun pointing out all the little gay bars and night clubs en route. They walked along the walking street and turned right into tapas alley. Alistair was really amazed. Oh, look at that window it looks gorgeous. Dozens of tapas bars were piling their windows high with dishes of Pintxos. The restaurants were preparing for the onslaught at 2pm for the Spanish locals and holiday makers to take their lunch. At the top Alistair said I want my lunch there. They were standing outside La Cava Aragonesa, one of the best tapas bars in town and always packed. Well we can, come on Renaldo said the hotels just up here on the right.

They spotted Cecil and Michael sitting at the bar as the windows around the hotel bar were floor to ceiling glass. Philippe the owner swept out from behind the bar and greeted them enthusiastically. Welcome my darlings come and have a drink at the bar, and I'll get Angelo to take your cases up to your room. Oh, thank you said Alistair giving Angelo an approving smile. They had big hugs with Cecil and Michael. What you 'avin said Mike. Whatever your drinking said Alistair. Two large vodkas and tonics please Phillipe. Coming up. Any ice? Oh, eye lots of ice said Mike, they're from the south they like to drown their drinks and they all laughed. Alistair downed his second large vodka at the Casa don Phillipe and was feeling a bit woozy, they'd been up to the room to freshen up, admired the small but chic accommodation. I'm feeling a bit hungry chaps, we thought we'd try that lovely little tapas bar around the corner for a spot of lunch will you join us? Yes, do said Renaldo. Oh, ok why not said Mike. We've had a huge breakfast said Cecil. So, tapas will be just the thing, I'm game. They drunk up and made their way around to the bar, They ordered a jug of sangria and then took it in turns to go up and point at the pintxos and snacks that they wanted, even Renaldo being Spanish couldn't make himself heard in the noisy bar so language wasn't a barrier you just pointed smiled and nodded. There was a lovely buzzy, happy atmosphere. Alistair now a bit pissed said I'll be honest guys I didn't like the idea of coming here really but from what I've seen so far, its delightful. Oh, you ain't seen nothing yet said Mike wait till we take you to GG's tonight.

Alistair awoke from his siesta feeling a bit groggy. Renaldo was still asleep. It was 7pm. He reached for his bottle of water and took two paracetamols. He could have stayed there all night, but he didn't want to be a killjoy. They had arranged to meet Mike and Cecil in the bar at 8pm. He poked Renaldo gently and said you had better wake up. Renaldo moaned and put his arm out to Alistair, what's the time? 7 o'clock said Alistair. Oh, good we have time said Renaldo pulling Alistair towards him. Much as I'd like to, I don't think I have the energy darling Alistair said. Pop the kettle on will you while I go and shower.

Mike and Cecil were up and out. Mike liked his tea at 6pm so they were down at Rays fish and chip shop. Mike had a large haddock, chips, baked beans and curry sauce. He liked the beans and curry sauce tipped over his chips. Cecil said he was uncouth. Mike said he didn't give a fook. Cecil had grilled Plaice and some bread and butter; he was still full up from lunch time. When they finished, they made their way back up the hill to the hotel and sat in the bar and waited for the other two. Did you bring condoms and the lube? said Mike. Yes, it's in my man bag all ready, and a bottle of poppers said Cecil. You can 'ave bottom th'end tonight he belched I'm too full. I should think so said Cecil bloody gannet.

Alistair and Renaldo made their way down to the bar. 'Ello lads what you 'avin said Mike? Oh, just a fizzy water for me said Alistair and I'll have a Cana said Renaldo a small beer. Water! Said Mike bloody water. Yes, for now that's enough thank you said Alistair.

Where are we going for dinner? said Alistair. Oh, we've already had us teas said Cecil, Mike likes to eat at 6pm otherwise he's up all night. Oh, ok said Alistair a bit bemused. I'm still full from lunchtime. We can grab a burger, or some churros later said Renaldo we will go out for a nice meal tomorrow. We thought we'd 'ave one 'ear said Mike then take a walk around maybe have one in the Hagar bar and the Intimate bar and then go up to GG's. Sounds good to me said Alistair.

They arrived at GG's at 10pm it was in full swing. Luchie was on the door. A 70 year old drag queen very famous in the Alicante region. He was the owner of the bar. He greeted Mike and Cecil warmly lots of hola's and kissing on both cheeks and they introduced him to Alistair and Renaldo. He kissed them both on the cheek and said welcome, he said something to Renaldo in Spanish and laughed. Renaldo went red and replied with something Alistair didn't catch. In fact, Renaldo had been here before quite a few times as a younger man. He had always liked the older man and had come here to meet them; however, he hadn't mentioned it to Alistair. Luchie quickly worked out the situation and winked broadly over Alistair's shoulder. Alistair paid the entrance fee for them all which was 40 Euros and he was a bit taken aback. Oh, that includes the first drink said Mike handing him 20 euros. It is fookin expensive, but you get a lot for your money, ee 'as to do that otherwise the Spanish men just come in to get a bit of the other, 'ave a dance then go. They don't drink much the Spanish and if they can get away with not paying owt they will. They made their way into this huge nightclub. Alistair was astounded there was a massive long bar with stools and then several leather

sofas dotted about. This lead through into another bar
with a dance floor where there looked to be about 30
couples all well past 60 dancing the pasadoble on the
dance floor with dozens of onlookers it was packed.
They each took a seat while Renaldo took the door
tickets up to the bar to exchange for drinks. Alistair
said how marvellous I haven't seen anything like this
before in all my life. Soon after a very handsome
young man approached their table. Typical Spanish
good looks big brown eyes, wavy hair a fit body, he
bent down and gave Mike then Cecil a kiss on the
cheek. This is Paco the one I was telling you about he
said as he introduced them to Alistair and Renaldo.
He's gorgeous said Alistair, fit too. Yes, he should be
he's in the Guardia civil, the police said Mike. Paco
joined them and soon he and Renaldo were jabbering
away in Spanish together. Soon it was time for
Luchie to do his show. This was a traditional
Flamenco show. He mimed to old female singers in
the cante jondo Andalusian gypsy style, big dramatic
numbers with lots of stamping of feet and twisting
movements he was great. As he started to swish
about the floor in a traditional flamenco dress with a
long train covered in turquoise ribbons and flowers
Mike said. Oh fook 'ere she goes I'm off. Don't you
like it said Alistair? No, I fookin don't said Mike all
that caterwauling. This is our time to head out the
back to the rest room with Paco if you don't mind.
Secretly shocked Alistair said no not at all, of course,
please do what you like, I'm enjoying the show. Mike
nodded to Paco and he got up with Cecil and
followed him out towards the back of the club to a
little cabin especially reserved for such activities.

Renaldo looked at Alistair and laughed, your face!
He said. I thought I'd seen it all in my youth said

Alistair I was obviously wrong. The show finished
and the dancers returned to the stage as it was Tango
time. They are quite marvellous aren't they said
Alistair, some are like professional dancers. Beats
strictly doesn't it laughed Renaldo. Come with me
there's more to see yet said Renaldo. Alistair
followed him thorough another arch were there was
rows and rows of chairs laid out like a meeting at the
local town hall in Peacehaven where Alistair used to
be a local councillor. But instead of looking at some
old dear's holiday slides these old dears here were
watching hard core gay porn. Oh, my word said
Alistair as he took a seat near the back. After five
minutes he said shall we go? Follow me said Renaldo.
You've been here before said Alistair wagging his
finger at Renaldo. They went out into another
corridor, one side lined with cabins some doors
locked some open. One guy in his 70's was laying
stark naked on a mattress playing with his cock and
beckoned them in. Oh no thank you said Alistair I'm
with someone. Renaldo laughed. From the end cabin
there came quite a lot of noise, lots of moaning and
groaning then they heard in a loud whisper. Oy! 'alf
time swap ends I fancy a go downt there. It was
Mikes undisguisable voice. On the left was a room,
pitch black, follow me said Renaldo hold my hand
and don't let go. As they walked through Alistair
realised this was obviously one of the dark rooms, he
had read about but never experienced. As they
walked into the pitch black space a hand reached out
and grabbed Alistair's crotch. Alistair gave a little
gasp, then another grabbed his arse and he felt
someone kissing his neck. Get me out of here now he
hissed at Renaldo. Renaldo pulled him back towards
the entrance. When they got outside Alistair said

angrily why did you take me in there it was revolting. Renaldo laughed, because you should experience everything once! He said. Do you want to go somewhere else? Yes, please somewhere quiet! I've had far too much excitement for one night. They made their way back through the dance area where a very energetic waltz was taking place. They got out of the front door and walked back towards the seafront where they found a little cafe and ordered a coffee and brandy each and sat and looked at the sea. WELL! said Alistair and then burst into laughter. He couldn't stop and it was infectious, they both had tears pouring down their faces recollecting the nights events.

Sunday Morning

John and Grant had finished work on the MP's roof and were having a few days off. Johns ex-wife Sarah was keeping James and Katy for the holiday and taking them down to her parent's place in Southend for the weekend. They were sitting in the garden as it was quite warm debating whether to go down to the pub and watch Daisy's Sunday school or not, they could hear a lot of banging and effing and jeffing coming from next door. John got up and looked over the fence. What's up Roz. Oh, I'm sorry I didn't know you were out there said Roz, that's alright laughed John what's wrong? Its these bleeding yurts Yo's bought they've come with no instructions. Hang on we'll pop round and give you a hand said John. No, it's your day off I'll manage. Its ok open the door.

100

Come on Grant Roz needs a hand. When they entered the garden, they said where's Yo then? Oh, she had a nasty experience a few days ago at school it shook her up badly. She's gone to a peace retreat somewhere in Cumbria to recover. Got any beers in the fridge then said Grant? sure, I'll go and get us all one said Roz. An hour later they had finished. Thank fuck for that said Roz. What are they for anyway said Grant? Oh, Yo's got it in her head to do BnB for the summer for vegi women. Grant said what in the garden. Well it's a big enough plot said Roz. Grant suddenly wished they hadn't been so helpful. Roz picked up on his anxiety. Don't worry boys it'll be a five minute wonder no doubt. There won't be any rave ups or parties it's just for meditation and all of that bollocks. John laughed you're not into it all then Roz. Na not me, I just go along with it all for a peaceful life. Well we're thinking of going down to the Fawcett Inn to watch the show, why don't you come with us? Can I? I'd love a pint and a roast dinner if you promise not to tell Yo? They both laughed of course not said Grant. I'll tell you what I'll treat you both for helping me how's that. Well thanks Roz that would be lovely. We will just go next door and freshen up. Righto I'll come around for you in 20 minutes. She's nice old Roz isn't she said John. Yes, said Grant, I think everyone likes Roz, shame that Yolanda can be such a pain in the arse sometimes though. John looked at Grant with pure lust in his eyes. Oy stop it said Grant, come on we've got 20 minutes laughed John, plenty of time. Roz rang on the door. Grant ran down to open the door not quite dressed. Come in a minute we are nearly ready. Roz smiled to herself she guessed what had been going on. 5 minutes later they both came down flushed but happy. When they got to the pub it was really busy, so they had a drink while they waited. Soon they were tucking into roast beef and Yorkshire pudding with all the trimmings. They watched the show. Daisy was off sick this week, so Allana Cardinal took over the top spot. Which didn't matter as he was very funny, and the crowd loved him nearly as much as Daisy. Only one act got through to the final, a dog act called "A friend of Dorothy's" This consisted of a big bear known to all as hairy Mary dressed up like Judy Garland in the wizard of Oz, even down to the ruby red slippers, and a dog called Toto who could do amazing dance tricks like Pudsey and Ashleigh in the real Britain's got talent. The crowd went mad when Hairy Mary and Toto did their little skip up the yellow brick road together.

6 hours later the three of them fell out of a taxi paralytic, after doing a huge pub crawl of all the bars in Kemp town. John was the worst of the three and Roz had to help Grant get him in the house. Still they had had a great day out. Roz had really enjoyed herself and let herself be herself for once.

Alistair and Renaldo had called it a day the night before at midnight and were up, and now walking down at the Levante beach. The other really long well-kept beach in Benidorm walking off the cobwebs by 9am. They managed to walk the complete 1.3 miles from one end to the other and back again. Stopping here and there for a coffee and a bit of breakfast. The weather was beautiful not a cloud in the sky and they sat and indulged in an hour or so people watching on the great stretch of beach. I know a lovely little spot not far from here where we can go for lunch said Renaldo shall we ask Mike and Cecil asked Renaldo. Yes do, I'm dying to find out what happened last night laughed Alistair.

They met the other guys after freshening up a bit back at the hotel. They walked down to the Parc de Elche to pick up the car. Do you two know La Cala de Finestrat? asked Renaldo. Yes, we do said Cecil we usually pop down there once while we are here. We know quite a few people down there. Really? said Alistair. Yes, said Mike a lot of the gays who live out here live down in the bay. They all drink at a bar called the Marina I'll take you there after lunch. Ok great said Alistair.

They parked up and walked over to a really pretty little bay, oh this is lovely said Alistair so pretty. Eye it is said Mike it's got a bit built up in some parts like everywhere, but the bay is lovely. They walked around to El Arenal restaurant which Renaldo knew, they walked past the Marina bar which was very busy, and Mike and Cecil waved at a few people sitting there. They had a splendid lunch, delicious salad followed by the biggest grilled sole (Lenguado) Alistair had ever seen. A couple of bottles of chilled rosado as they gazed out to sea and they were feeling no pain. It was heavenly thought Alistair. After lunch they made their way back to the Marina bar. A couple waved at Mike and Cecil and beckoned them over, there was now a huge crowd of people sitting there with all the tables pushed together. There must have been 30 of them. Gary and Mike the friends of Cecil's and Mike did the introductions and Alistair realised he knew two of them, Jeremy and Colin from Brighton. Within seconds the waiter Jesus had added another table to the crowd and soon they were chatting to the gang and the drinks never stopped coming. Renaldo decided to leave the car until the morning and got stuck in with the rest of them. They had so much fun and laughed so much with this lively crowd. They were a mixed bunch, mainly gay men but a few straight couples and a couple of glamorous single women on their own. One or two of the guys were clearly past their sell by date early thought Alistair as one of them slumped forward head on the table, but after a nap he woke up and called out for another one for the road. Before they even knew it, the time was 10 o'clock at night. It was still warm, and they had had a ball.

Bank holiday Monday

Fat Gemma had dragged his huge suitcase down to The Fawcett Inn on the bus and hurled it up the stairs to Marys flat. Fooking 'ell what ave you got in there? 'ave you weighed that bastard said Mary? No said Gemma. You can't take all that luv said Mary come on, get one of the boys up to help you weigh it, you'll get fined for being overweight luv. I didn't think said Gemma. Eye and I never thought to tell you said Mary. Better to sort it out now than at airport. Ave you got yer passport. Yes, I've got it said Gemma. Thank fook for that Mary said. Earlier in the week it suddenly dawned on Gemma that he didn't have a passport. Dolly had driven him up to London and spent all day at the passport office diving in a booth to quickly get some passport photos taken.

Gemma and Mary were both working the lunchtime

session. Then they were meeting the others in the bar at 6pm to have a few drinks to get them in the mood, then the minibus Mary had booked was picking them up at 9pm to take them up to Gatwick. Their flight wasn't until midnight, but they all wanted to have a few drinks at the airport and a meal before the flight.

AT 6pm Tina tits and Harry Harrington were the first through the door in matching outfits. White jeans and very loud Hawaiian short sleeved shirts topped off with matching panama hats. Fook me said Mary you look like the two out of La cage aux folles laughed Mary. The touring version laughed Gemma. Who rattled your cage dear said Harry scornfully, have you looked in the mirror dear? You look like Chris Biggins in drag. Thanks a bunch, said Gemma brushing the insult off, he was so excited he could hardly contain himself. Next in was Dolly, she looked absolutely beautiful, in a cream and black Chanel two piece topped off with a black 1970s floppy Biba hat and Jackie O sunglasses. The others gave her a round of applause. Thank you, darlings, she said in her deep voice. A large gin please Olly who was standing in for Mary and whatever everyone else wants. Pissy Michael was in next followed by Larry. Have you put those special pants on Michael? said Mary. Yes, Mary said Michael embarrassed. Good don't want you pissing on the seat like last time luv do we. The others pretended not to hear. By the time the minibus arrived they were all in the holiday mood very jolly with lots of banter going backwards and forwards. They made a pretty sight at the check in desk at Gatwick. All sporting their 'Barley Tours' badges that Mary had made them all wear for a joke in case they got lost.

After what seemed like a lifetime, they arrived at the hotel in Benidorm at 3.30 am. All tired out and over refreshed. Mary booked alarm calls for 9am so they would all get up for breakfast and arranged to meet them around the pool in the morning. Gemma too excited to sleep poured them two vodkas and oranges from the minibar. Getting undressed Mary waved a panty liner at Gemma and said look at that dear, dry as a bone, not a fuckin drop. Not bad for a woman of my age Gemma luv. Gemma didn't know whether to be sick or laugh. Instead he pulled on his nightie and got into the next bed. I 'ope you don't fooking snore said Mary as she pulled on her eye mask.

Ben had taken a week's holiday from work, he wanted to re access his life. He was quite ashamed of taking payment in the form of sex and cocaine. In fact, he knew deep down that his love of cocaine was what had led him to go down that route. It made him feel invincible and he loved that feeling of power too that came with it. The comedown after it though was terrible, and the last few times of excess had left him feeling morbidly depressed. He looked over at Gordon who was laying on the sofa thumbing his way through Country life magazine, Ben put down his Guardian and said, how do you fancy going away for a few days, I'm due some leave, when said Gordon? Tomorrow said Ben. Tomorrow? I can't just take time off like that said Gordon. Well except for being ill with your bum problem you've not had a holiday for a year, ring into work and make some excuse. Tell them you've got to go to a funeral in Ireland and you need the rest of the week off. Make something up, use your imagination for once said Ben sounding tetchy. I need a break. Well where do you want to go? I don't know, Valencia? I'd love to go there said Gordon I've heard its really chic now. Right, well go and get online and pick a nice hotel, run it past me, if I approve, I'll let you book the flights. Ok I'll get onto it said Gordon. Half an hour later he called Ben into the office, come and have a look at these, I've picked two.

Ben went into the office; they both look nice. One was ultra-modern and cool in the new fashionable museum-gallery part of town, the other was an old established 5 star hotel, where the Spanish Royal family stayed. Gordon had his fingers crossed under the desk. I suppose you want the grand one said Ben, Gordon nodded enthusiastically. Go on then book that then, you're such a bloody snob Gordon, and you're not thought Gordon but didn't say anything, He booked the hotel, the five star Palacio Vallier. He booked a suite; he deserved a treat. Unfortunately, flights were proving tricky. There was a Ryan air flight in the morning, Gordon quickly discounted that, Easy jet were full, there were a few seats on a British airways flight, but the flight was quite late 6pm Oh well thought Gordon at least we will get there in one piece and booked it.

Ok it's done lets pack said Gordon excitedly. He had rung into work and told the funeral story, nobody believed him, but it wasn't that busy and nothing was said. Ben got the cases out of the loft; Gordon ran up to the dungeon and grabbed a few of his favourite toys just in case and put them in a spare toilet bag. They spent two hours going through the wardrobe picking out and then discarding clothes. Eventually they were ready, hand luggage sorted. Come on let's open that bottle of Pol Roger champagne that's left over in the fridge since Christmas said Gordon. Go on then said Ben his mood was perking up now he knew he was getting away.

Yolanda yawned and gave Roz a peck on the cheek, she had driven back from her retreat and had fallen into a deep sleep on the sofa. Roz ruffled her hair. Cup of tea? Oh yes please said Yo, she strolled out into the garden and did a little yelp of delight when she saw the yurts. Roz came out clutching two mugs of tea, Oh Roz thank you darling said Yo, what a lovely surprise. Roz went a bit pink blushing. I've been busy on my retreat working on my new website for my BnB said Yo. I thought you went away for a rest said Roz. Oh, I did darling it was wonderful but, in the evening, I did that. It was so nice and quiet, no stress, I think I've put together a nice design, I'll show you later. Ok said Roz I've been thinking about this shower business. Grant said him and John will come in and fix up the plumbing. Really! said Yo that's so kind of them. They are nice guys said Roz they actually came in and helped me yesterday to get the yurts up properly. Did they? God I'm surprised, they voted for Brexit you know? Roz went red and changed the subject quickly, she'd secretly voted for Brexit too. What do you fancy for dinner then? said Roz.

TUESDAY

Gemma and Mary were downstairs for breakfast at 9.15. They had helped themselves to the enormous buffet and Gemma was looking around in wonderment. Oh, Mary thanks for asking me, I can't believe it it's like a dream. Your welcome darlin you'll fooking luv Benidorm dear I promise. They had already staked out their sunbeds and threw their bags and bits on a few other beds for the others when they finally made it down to the pool area.

Mary and Gemma had got oiled up and were laying back on their sunbeds soaking the rays. After 10 minutes Gemma couldn't stand it anymore and dragged his sunbed behind Mary's and got in the shade. Oh, Mary it's so hot said Gemma, well of course it is you silly cont, it's Spain luv. Now lay behind me if you like but tuck your balls in those shorts you look a right pratt with you knackers hanging out. Gemma puffed and panted a bit then settled down with a copy of Take a break.

Next down was Dolly, Mary spotted her, and she gave her a wave, over ere luv yelled Mary. Dolly just glided along the side of the pool resplendent in a white flowing chiffon day coat gold sandals the Biba hat and Jackie O glasses. Behind her was a waiter holding a tray above his head with a large bottle of the local Larios gin some tonics and ice.

Morning girls said Dolly how are we all this morning? Great thanks said Mary, too hot said Gemma. Dolly sat down on the sunbed next to Mary, Señora where would you like this? Oh, put that on this table here, the waiter put a glass down on the pool table, no not that darling leave the bottle please. Que? Said Miguel the waiter. Dolly took 2 50 Euro notes out of her bag. Here you are Miguel, now put the bottle down por favor and keep the change. Oh, and bring some more glasses and extra ice please.

Si Senora, of course anything you want, he gave her a leering smile. Dolly pulled her Jackie O's down over the bridge of her nose. She gave him the once over. Not bad she thought, now hurry up there's a good boy she said in her deep husky voice, Miguel's face lit up, he poured them all a drink winked at Dolly and left. He fancies you said Mary, do you think? laughed Dolly. Yes of course he does, mind you that tip you just gave him would have made anyone smile. Still if you fancy a holiday fook, He'll give you one. Dolly laughed oh Mary really. They were just saying cheers when Tina tits and Harry arrived. Morning ladies said Harry, we just made breakfast, Larry and Michael are still in there. Pull those beds up said Mary I've saved them for you. Oh, ta said Tina I can't wait to lay down again. Tina just pulled off his T shirt and laid straight down on the sunbed. Fook me your tits are bigger than mine Tina said Mary. You wanna get some cream on those buggers they'll be sore and hold 'em up or you'll get white lines underneath Mary giggled. Tina pretended not to hear. Harry removed his T shirt and then shorts revealing a pink thong. Oh, dear your taking a risk with that on said Mary, why? said Harry, well you're a bit old now luv aren't you. Your arse is sagging a bit isn't it. Bloody cheek said Harry. Let's all 'ope you don't shit yerself luv, I'm not being rude darlin I'm just telling the truth. Well lie laughed Harry. I don't mean no 'arm luv, it's just my bit of fun said Mary.

Next out of the trap were Larry and pissy Michael, they got the two end sunbeds, Michael thin as a rake and pasty white, his metal framed glasses steaming up just sat on the end of his chatting to Tina. Larry stripped off down to a pair of Speedo budgie smugglers. Fooking Nora said Mary, Dolly 'ave a look. Dolly glanced over and choked on her gin. Jesus said Dolly that cannot be real. Harry sat up and had a look. Oh, look at that, it's like a baby's arm holding an orange. Oh, where's me fan I've come over all hot. I told you it was big said Tina. I would never 'ave got it in me gob if I hadn't 'ave taken me teeth out. Yes, on the floor of the pub you dirty cont said Mary. Larry headphones in was oblivious to the others gossip he oiled up what was a pretty good body for a 49 year old. Nicely toned and firm all over. Drinks boys? said Dolly calling Miguel over, I've got gin here, but I can get you a beer or something. I'll have a champagne cocktail please said Harry, the others had beers. Mary said now you be careful how many beers you have Michael. Why? I'm on my holiday said Michael. I know that darlin but make sure you don't piss in the bloody pool ok luv? the toilets are over there. Dolly got her purse out again and paid for the drinks. You can't keep doin that darlin said Mary, what? said Dolly, paying for all the drinks said Mary. Don't worry I've got plenty said Dolly. You're a good sort Dolly but I'm no ponce luv, we'll 'ave a kitty, 20 euros in each everybody she yelled is that ok? Dolly's not payin' for all the drinks all 'olliday right! That's fair said Harry. They all got their money out. We'll keep to this all week and that way those who are a bit slow at putting their 'and in their pocket won't get away with it ok, she said looking directly at pissy Michael.

And so for the next few hours it carried on, lots of banter too many drinks, a flustered Miguel, a heat fatigued and slightly pissed Gemma a lot of laughter and a good time was being had by all, even if they did get a few funny looks from some of the other guests. Fook 'em darlin's, said Mary they can't talk, I've never seen so many ugly fat fookin' bastards in all of me life.

Around 4.30pm they all decided to go for a siesta, all at different levels of dishevelment. As they were half board they arranged to meet in the hotel bar at 7.30pm for cocktails. Being a Tuesday night, they decided to stay in the new town and had a lot of fun going around the different clubs watching various tribute acts. Like "Fake that" An Elvis who had seen much better days, A lousy mime drag show (haven't seen one of them for bloody years said Mary) Plus to round it off. Sticky Vicky's magic strip show, where Vicky (an illusionist) was able to pull a whole christmas tree including flashing lights out of her vagina. Harry looked like he was going to be sick. Dolly just watched in total amazement speechless. The others thought it was a hoot including pissy Michael who laughed so hard the inevitable happened and they all decided to call it a night and head for home. When they came out of the bar, the heavens had opened and there was a terrific electric storm overhead. The rain was bucketing it down. Oh, fooking ell said Mary fook this boys lets go back inside until it's over.

Tuesday was Josh and Franks day off usually but with Mary and Gemma away they hung around to make sure everything ran smoothly; Olly was on the bar. Wendy wrap was in the kitchen. Josh watched Wendy with the lunch orders and got stuck in with her for a bit until she was more confident. It wasn't busy. They had also roped in old Bernard one of the regulars, a retired bus driver to help with the washing up. Once the rush was over, they rushed around to the Sallis Benny theatre at the university which had kindly offered them some rehearsal room so they could work on the bandit boyz songs and dance routines. Josh had hired a dance instructor an ex "west end Wendy" (chorus boy) called Randy now turned choreographer to put the boys through their paces. They had the rest of the day to work with them.

All were present and correct. Harry played it cool and didn't let on that he was seeing Josh and Frank. They lined up and Randy just let them dance freestyle to see how they moved. They were good. Your all terrible said Randy. Fuck knows how I'm going to turn you lot into dancers I don't know. The boys all looked dejected. Well they are going to work hard aren't you guys said Josh. They all nodded.

Randy got up on stage and showed them some moves he wanted them to copy. They were pretty quick but not coordinated. It would take time and hours of rehearsal to lick them into shape thought Josh but as he said to Frank, they have definitely got the sex factor eh? After a break Randy got ready to leave saying to Josh quietly, they are good, get them up on their vocals and they will be something special. Right I'm off yelled Randy you were all shit I want you to practice every spare minute you've got, wherever you are, got it? Yes, Randy said the boys.

Afterwards they all went for a pizza again and although exhausted they were pretty fired up. Harry looked at Frank and winked when no one was looking.

Josh explained that they needed to meet twice a week at the theatre for rehearsal and that they must try and practice at home or in Jacks parents' garage as much as possible.

He sympathised that they had day jobs. Harry worked for his dad as a plumber he was already doing a lot of online study as well as the practical for that. Jack was learning the jewellery business from his family and worked as a salesman in one of the jeweller's shops in the Lanes. Sam was a self-employed painter and decorator. So, it was going to be hard, but they were all up for it.

Frank dropped Jack and Sam off first, Harry being the last, He pulled up outside Harry's house and said. Well, we will see you soon young man. Guys I've got a problem said Harry. What's wrong said Josh. Harry pointed down to his crotch, his hardon was bursting through the fabric of his grey Adidas trackies. Josh laughed, what are you like. Can't I come home with you guys? We were just gonna stream a movie from Netflix tonight said Frank we're knackered after the bank holiday weekend mate. Oh well change of plan by the look of it said Josh, come on then back to the Crescent it is.

Yolanda was hard at it at the computer refining her new website to advertise her BnB it was called HMW which stood for Hera Meditation Workshop (a sanctuary for Women only) Hera being the Greek goddess of women.

The website blurb read as follow.

HMW is a specially designed retreat strictly for vegan women including vegan Trans women only.

Join me and my partner Roz for a quiet break by the seaside in Brighton.

We offer Two self-catering Yurts in our pretty organic garden which sleep up to 4 women in each Yurt. You will receive an ethically sourced vegan breakfast hamper including a selection of herbal teas and non-dairy milk products and organic cereals that you can prepare at your leisure. Each yurt has a solar panelled heating stove for you to boil a kettle for drinks. We will provide you with towels and non-biological shower gel, so you can use our newly installed fresh rainwater outside shower facility. There is a toilet for your use inside the house.

Please bring your own yoga mats. Classes + meditation sessions will be held every morning at 9am and every evening at sundown.

We also offer a safe space in the garden if you need to reflect or feel the need for some solitude. There are also some beautiful walks close by across the Sussex downs and of course there is the beach.

There are many vegetarian restaurants in Brighton for the evenings as well as bongo drum workshops, Art classes, Drama groups, feminist out-reach groups, even African tribal dance classes. So much fun you won't know where to start.

Prices are £300 per night per yurt based on four women sharing.

Please contact me Yolanda at....................

What do you think she asked Roz who was peering over her shoulder? Great but don't get me too involved, this is your gig remember? And don't you think £300 a night is stronging it a bit? No, it's only £75per head. It costs £100 minimum a night now in some of those dumps in town. Besides, I shall use my contacts, our guests will be mostly from Islington or Camden, professional women with more money than sense. Well that's not very Marxist is it said Roz laughing. Yo went red, what I mean is those women think nothing of spending £100 on lunch so £75 a night for BnB is nothing, in fact I'm practically giving it away. Yo was feeling positively philanthropic.

Gordon and Ben were chilling out in the British airway's VIP lounge at Gatwick, there had just been an announcement that their flight would be delayed by 1 hour until 7pm. Ben was not happy. Why didn't you book easy jet he asked Gordon? Because they were full Gordon replied. Mmm go and get me another drink and get me some food said Ben. Eventually they boarded and were on their way to Valencia. They were about 30 mins from landing when the captain announced that the seatbelt sign would be going on as they were expecting to experience some turbulence. The captain said would all crew members please return to their seats. Ben sighed as they strapped up, just then he saw a flash of lightening outside of his window and the plane tipped over to the right. Then the plane started bumping about all over the place. Gordon grabbed Ben's hand and held it tight. Jesus that was close said Ben. A few minutes later it happened again everyone was hurled forwards in their seats. Ben grabbed the headrest of the seat in front of him and braced himself. The plane was rocking and rolling now and some of the passengers were screaming. The captain said. I've decided for your safety that we are not going to try and land at Valencia as it seems that the storm is at its worst over there, I am going to turn around and land in Alicante. Everyone please stays in your seats.

Eventually after another half an hour of circling Alicante in what was a terrible storm, the captain got a slot and was allowed to land in Alicante. Apparently, Valencia airport had had to shut as part of the building had been struck by lightning. They then had to sit on the plane for another 30 minutes while the airport arranged coaches and baggage handlers out to the plane to bring them inside.

There were some very irate passengers yelling and shouting. How are we supposed to get to Valencia from here? I've got a car waiting for me in Valencia. Eventually the captain said. British airways has arranged for coaches to be laid on outside of Alicante airport to bus you to Valencia. A big cheer went up. When they disembarked, they asked where they were supposed to get the coaches from and were told to wait in one of the empty lounges for further instructions. After 2 hours there was still no sign of the coaches. A very flustered British airways rep was trying his best to field off the angry passengers. Eventually he made an announcement. British airways are willing to offer you hotel vouchers for one night at a local hotel and then help you with your onward journey in the morning. Because of the storm some roads are closed and the coaches that we booked for you haven't arrived. However, there are enough taxis outside to take you to a hotel. We have arranged for accommodation in two hotels that have vacancies. There is one hotel here at the airport and one in Benidorm that can take us. Those with children will get priority to stay here at the hotel the rest will have to go into Benidorm. Please form an orderly queue at the desk. I don't fucking believe this said Ben. When they got to the front of the queue, the rep said I've only got room left now for Benidorm. We don't want to go to bloody Benidorm said Gordon horrified. I'm afraid that's all we've got said Simon. your welcome to try and make your own way to Valencia of course or arrange your own accommodation somewhere else if you prefer but there are trees down on the main A7 road to Valencia and it getting late, it was now close to 2am. Are you two from Brighton said Simon, Yes why? Said Ben I thought I recognised you from the Subline club said Simon. Look he whispered do yourselves a favour take the hotel in Benidorm its 4 star and really nice. The one at the airport here is a shit hole, anyway you'll be better off in Benidorm. Ok that'll have to do said Ben looking at Simon, he was quite cute. Actually, our crew can't get back now, and we've all got to rest and we're all opting to go to Benidorm too. Well I refuse to stay in Benidorm I'd sooner sleep in here said Gordon pouting. Really said Ben then bloody stay here I'm going to the hotel. See you later. Simon handed over the voucher to Ben and couldn't get over the size of Ben's hands. He gave Ben that look and said maybe see you there later for a night cap. You never know said Ben. Gordon looked at him furiously. Are you coming said Ben? Gordon nodded. Good well get the cases then and load them on a trolley and push them to the taxi rank. See you later he said to Simon winking.

They handed the address to the taxi driver and he said. Ah hotel Helios very nice place. You lucky.

They arrived at the Hotel about 50 minutes later. Gordon was sobbing quietly in the back, look at this place it's like hell on earth said Gordon. Look at that lot down there staggering up the road all drunk. I knew it would be full of common people he whimpered. Look its only for one night said Ben let's get to bed it's all your fucking fault anyway. They made their way into reception and were surprised by the modern stylish décor. Oh, this isn't so bad said Ben. The night receptionist was very sympathetic to their story and said he would get their room sorted as quickly as possible. He was just handing them their room key when Gordon heard a familiar voice behind him say. Fook me what are you two doin' ere? Ben and Gordon turned around and there was Mary Barley pissed as a newt surrounded by a bunch of drunks, they recognised from The Fawcett Inn but would never dream of mixing with. Oh, dear god said Gordon this can't get any worse. They pretended they hadn't seen them and headed for the lift ignoring the Brightonian's. Stuck up pair of cont's said Mary, come on bed everyone. Larry make sure Michael gets stripped off and wipe him down for god's sake. I'm not his bloody carer said Larry. He paid for your fooking room luv said Mary it's the least you can do dear. See ya all tomorrow around the pool.

Ben and Gordon let themselves into their room. This is very nice said Ben. Gordon said I can't believe all those bloody plebs are here. Oh, stop moaning and get to bed. Ben hung his clothes up and got his toilet bag out went into the bathroom and took a shower. When he had finished Gordon went in to the same. Ben walked over to the mini bar and opened the door, but it was empty, of alcohol anyway just cokes and water. He pulled on some lounge pants and a top and yelled out to Gordon. I'm just popping downstairs see if I can get us a couple of drinks from the bar. Ok yelled Gordon a bit more cheerful now the hot shower was working its magic.

Ben strolled along to the lift. Eventually he heard the ping warning the lift was arriving. As the door opened there stood Simon in his blue blazer and overnight wheelie bag. Well there's a nice surprise said Simon. Ben laughed what floor do you want said Simon he was staring at Ben's crotch, his cock was flopping about inside his lounge pants, whatever floor you're on said Ben grabbing Simons hand and rubbing it on his now stiff cock.

Gordon was laying on the bed trying to connect his phone to the hotel Wi-Fi, but he couldn't get a signal. Where the hell was Ben? He sorted through his flight bag and got a book out and his eye mask and ear plugs plus a jar of Lancôme night cream he had bought on the plane and got into bed. After 45 minutes he thought where the fuck is, he. Jumping out of bed and pulling his jogging bottoms on and a tight white T shirt muttering to himself he said, I bet he's in the bar chatting up the barman the fucker. He grabbed the door key and went out and got the lift down to the bar. Walking up to the night receptionist. He said excuse me where is the bar please? Its closed señor I'm sorry. But my partner came down to get a drink said Gordon. I've not seen him señor but maybe he slipped out to one of the late bars down the road, although your too late now for Sticky Vicky. What's Sticky Vicky said Gordon incredulously. The famous female stripper who pulls the christmas tree from her how you say in English her wanny. Yes, that's it her wanny. Gordon thought he was going to faint. You are joking right? said Gordon no senor she's very good even has the er illuminations. How disgusting said Gordon heading back to the lift. He was right this was hell on earth alright. As he reached his floor, he was walking down the long corridor back to his room thinking I'll text Ben maybe the barman got it wrong. Just then a door opened, and Larry walked straight out in front of him carrying an ice bucket and wearing just a pair of Calvin Klein briefs.

Sorry mate said Larry as they nearly collided, I was just going over there to the ice machine, Gordon was about to berate him when he looked down and saw the size of Larry's lunch box. Oh, that's alright it was my fault said Gordon I should have watched where I was going. Hey, I know you, don't I? said Larry I don't think so said Gordon admiring Larry's fit body and tattoos. Yes, I've seen you in Brighton said Larry. Fancy a night cap? Er no I shouldn't really said Gordon then looking down again said oh go on then why not. Would you mind going over and getting some ice for me said Larry thrusting the ice bucket into Gordon's hands. Er no ok said Gordon. Larry rushed back into the room, grabbed the bed cover and threw it over Michael now dead to the world and covered him up from head to toe. Next, he turned out the lights except the one in the bathroom. He laid back on the bed with his hands behind his head. They never had the drink. Gordon was down on his knees in seconds. He couldn't believe the size of Larry's cock. It was jaw breaking. Larry eventually pulled him up from the floor and managed with difficulty to roll on top of Gordon. He kissed Gordon with such a passion Gordon thought he would pass out. Larry flipped him over, as Larry entered him with such force the pain, he experienced he converted into pleasure as his brain was able to do. Larry fucked him long and hard and when he came, he made quite a lot of noise. He collapsed on top of Gordon panting for breath, just then they heard a quiet little round of applause. Michael had woken up and watched the whole thing. Gordon looked over and saw the bathroom light reflecting from Michaels glasses he could just make out his face. Gordon screamed Oh dear god who the hell is that what's he doing there?

Larry laughed oh that's only Michael my roommate.
Go back to sleep you old pervert said Larry. Right oh
said Michael. Sorry about that mate I thought he was
asleep said Larry. Nearly gave me a heart attack said
Gordon he looks like the ghost of Charles Hawtrey.
Larry laughed yeah; I suppose he does a bit.
Incredible thought Gordon as he pulled his clothes on.
He made his way back to the room after a parting kiss
from Larry and a pat on the bum. He jumped into bed
still no Ben. He turned the light out.

On the floor above a similar scene had been carried
out with Ben and Simon. Ben had taken it easy and
they had just had normal but passionate sex. Ben
thought actually that it was quite nice for a change.
Role Play could be exhausting. He stared down at the
blonde head laying on his chest and stroked Simons
hair. Shame you have to go to Valencia tomorrow
said Simon, I could be here for another two days
before the airline sort out where I've got to go next.
Really said Ben thoughtful. Would you really like me
to stay? You bet said Simon reaching down and
taking Ben's hard again cock in his mouth. I'll see
what I can do said Ben pushing hard down on the
back of Simons Head.

Thirty minutes later he crept back into the room.
Gordon still awake heard him, get a drink, then did
you? Yeah eventually said Ben. Nice bar is it? said
Gordon. Actually, it was closed but there was a bar
next door open. You could have texted me to come
and join you said Gordon. Oh no it was truly awful
you would have hated it. Did you get me a drink?
said Gordon. No, no take outs allowed said Ben now
shut up and go to sleep. Gordon was seething but
then he remembered Larry's big cock and that kiss,

and he drifted off to sleep with a smile on his face. That'll teach the fucker he thought as he drifted off. Ben was working out a way he could delay their, departure.

In the morning Gordon woke up feeling rather sore and then remembered last night's encounter with Larry he could feel himself getting a hard on. Just then he heard a moan from Ben who was in the other bed, a twin bedded room the only type available. He said what's the matter. I've got terrible stomach ache said Ben, I've been up half the night didn't you hear me? No, I didn't. What's given you that then? I grabbed a burger from a kebab shop around the corner last night it must be that. Oh, and you didn't get me one? said Gordon. Well if you would prefer to have the shits rather than me fine shouted Ben. Gordon went silent. Then said I'm starving, let's go down for breakfast and then we had better pack so we can get out of this shithole ASAP. I can't travel like this said Ben, No I'm going to phone down to reception and see if we can stay another night or two. What said Gordon are you mad? I'm not staying here for another two days. Suit yourself said Ben go to Valencia then, leave me here dying. You know I can't drive over here said Gordon. Get a bus said Ben. I can't stay here in this dump its hell on earth. Oh, it's all about you as usual isn't it said Ben, Poor Gordon, not posh enough for you, you think you are better than all these people who save up all year to come and have a bit of sunshine. No, I don't protested Gordon Yes you do! for fucks sake go down and get

123

some breakfast take your beach bag with you and go and lay around the pool or go for a walk and get me some more Imodium. Stay out of my sight until I text you. I've hardly had a wink of sleep I need to catch up, maybe if I can get some rest and some fucking peace, we will move to Valencia tomorrow. Ok said Gordon contritely should I ask reception to get a doctor. I don't need a fucking doctor I just need a few hours' sleep, now piss off. Gordon went in the bathroom cleaned his teeth, grabbed his beach gear and left Ben to sleep. He got the lift down to reception and followed the signs to the restaurant.

Ben grabbed his phone and texted Simon. Morning babe are you awake? Simon texted straight back yes; I've just showered; ok I'll be right up said Ben.

Gordon walked into the dining room, A very cheerful girl called Paula welcomed him and explained the service. Gordon was impressed as he walked around the buffet area, he could see every type of breakfast imaginable available, He started with fresh orange juice and helped himself to coffee. After a delicious breakfast of fresh fruits, cereal and scrambled eggs with wholemeal toast and honey he was feeling more human, cheerful even. He strolled out into the pool area where there was a nice garden and a pool bar and still lots of empty sunbeds and got one that was in the sun. Fuck Ben he thought.

Before he went up to see Simon, he rang down to reception booked another night which was lucky as the receptionist explained we have had only one cancellation for tonight otherwise we are full. Great said Ben. Can I order room service? Yes, sir. Can you deliver to room 606 a bottle of your best Cava fresh orange juice, some fruit and breakfast selections enough for two please? But your room is 504 sir, yes but I want to surprise a friend, said Ben. Ok sir but it will take about an hour I'm afraid. That's ok in fact that's perfect said Ben.

Gordon had got himself oiled up and was listening to a classical selection he had made up on his Spotify playlist and was chilling nicely until he heard a bit of laughter and sunbeds being dragged about. Oh, Jesus it was that naff crowd from Brighton and who was that with them Larry? Oh god it was Larry what's he doing with them thought Gordon. Larry saw him and waved. Gordon feigned sleep. 10 minutes later Larry strolled over and sat on the sunbed next to Gordon. Morning mate I thought that was you. Oh, hi said Gordon I didn't see you over there he lied. What are you doing on your own said Larry? Gordon explained about Ben being sick. Oh, that's awful, poor lad. Let me go over there and grab my towel and things and I'll come and lay with you if you would like? said Larry. What about your friends? said Gordon. Oh, they won't mind I don't take much notice of them really, all that camping about gets on my tits a bit to be honest, ok that would be nice said Gordon.

Kris and Karl were getting excited they had been on the internet all day and finally booked a lavish marquee for the summer ball. It was really a wedding marquee, but it didn't matter it could seat 200 people plus there was a big dance floor, room for a stage and there was a vaulted ceiling full of sparkling lights and big beautiful chandeliers hanging from the centre points too. Oh, it's so gorgeous said Kris but it's very expensive don't you think we should ask the others first. No fuck them said Karl if the mean buggers don't chip in, I'll pay for it myself. You can't do that said Kris. Yes, I can, I've got a bit of money put away that my dad left me. I'll use that. We are hosting this ball and I'm going to make sure it'll be the best there can be. No one's going to say the Royal Sisters don't know how to throw a bash.

John and Grant were at the MPs house in Hove, luckily, he was up in London today for Primeminister's questions, so they had the house to themselves. They were eyeing up the extension, they were getting on well with it and the new bi folding doors would arrive soon. It's going to look great said Grant. Everything is top spec gonna cost a pretty penny. He's loaded said John they say MP's don't earn much, but you know why he asks for receipts for every little thing don't you. Yep I know it's going in for expenses at Westminster said Grant. You think he would have learned his lesson from the MP's expense scandal a few years back. He doesn't give a fuck that one said John he's a career politician, a champagne socialist, never done a day's work in his life, the horrible cunt. Grant said come on, back to work, as he got up, he knocked what was left of his coffee over and it was working its way towards a laptop on the island they had been sitting at. Shit quick grab that John, John grabbed the laptop and as he touched it the screen lit up and a video clip started playing. Well I never laughed John, come and get a load of this. Jesus said Grant there was Paul Bryan MP in all his glory naked except for a pair of fishnet stockings, on his knees going down on a man whose trousers were round his ankles in fact the man was very short so Paul was nearly on his elbows, the man getting the BJ was filming Paul giving him a full polish. The phone was a bit shaky, but they could see down the cistern of the lavatory pan and in clear black ink it said property of the House of Commons. The man shot his load over Paul's face and handed the phone back to Paul and said turn that off quickly. But Paul didn't, as the man bent down to pull his pants and trousers back up the camera caught his face full on. Fuck me is that who I think it is said Grant. Ha it sure is said John, Wally Burke, a very prominent member of the house of commons. Jesus fancy leaving that lying about said Grant I wonder what he intends to do with it? John plugged his phone into the laptop and started clicking away on the laptop. What are you doing said Grant? Investing in our pension said John. What? you can't do that said Grant. Who can't? Listen I'm still a Battersea boy at heart, I came up the hard way, this cunt has done nothing. This filth is worth a fortune to the right person, I bet there's a load more stuff on here too. I don't want anything to do with it said Grant. I can't believe you are transferring files from him even if he is a wanker. Don't watch then said John smacking his lips and rubbing his hand together.

Mary and Dolly were giggling away and joking with each other. Dolly looked divine in a white one piece Chanel swimsuit and her Biba hat and Jackie O's. Mary less so in a leopard skin one piece, a white towelling turban and gold mules with diamante trim. She wouldn't have looked out of place in Miami beach thought Dolly. Look at them two over there, very friendly aren't they said Mary. Very friendly indeed said Dolly, glancing over at Gordon and Larry. Gemma come over here and rub some oil on me back will you luv said Mary. Gemma hauled himself off of the sunbed now a vivid shade of pink. Gemma squatted down on his haunches. Blimey Gemma your tits are bigger than Dolly's said Mary are you sure you've not had them done? 'Ere Tina Mary yelled, Gemma 'eres gonna give you a run for yer money with his knockers dear. They all laughed. No, I'm quite happy as a man really, I just like dressing up as a woman, it makes me feel more confident somehow said Gemma.

Did I hear you talking about my décolletage? Mary Barley said Dolly, no luv, I was talking about your tit's luv that's all. You've got a fabulous pair of knockers for your age Dolly. Thank you dear my husband loved them said Dolly. May he rest in peace said Mary at least he left you well off though darlin'. Well yes but I was a wealthy woman in my own right. Did you get bullied at school much Gem said Dolly changing the subject. Oh yes, all the time, I was always the fattest kid in the class said Gemma. I'd get beaten up every night on the bus home. Even now I get called all sorts on me way home. Tell Dolly if you know their names luv said Mary. Dolly'll get 'em beaten up luv. She was married to a gangster weren't you Dolly! Well I don't think now is the time or place said Dolly, but Mary was in full flow. Dolly's mother Gemma was a very successful landlady, she had a big pub in the east end of London didn't she Dolly, er yes but, Dolly grew up with the Kray twins and all those villains, didn't you Dolly, I don't think Gemma will know who.... She used to go round to the Kray's house for a cup of tea when she was little girl didn't you Dolly Aunty Vera's wasn't it? said Mary. Aunty Violet actually said Dolly exasperated. So, if you need anyone fookin' kneecapped ask Dolly said Mary. Gemma looked dumbstruck.

Is that all true? said Harry Harrington looking at

Dolly with a newfound respect. Yes, sort of said Dolly but it was all a long time ago I was only a little girl really said Dolly. But you married a villain said Tina sitting up on his hand. I did said Dolly giving up now, my mother went bloody mad I can tell you. She'd paid for me to go to private school and I had elocution lessons, the lot, and then I married Freddie. Mummy said I've only ever wanted what was best for you Dolly, but I thought that you'd marry a lawyer or a doctor or something. Fred is the best mum I said I love him. Yes, but the best bleeding bank robber in London was not what I had in mind my mother said. They all burst out laughing including Dolly. Oh, fuck it any one fancy a drink she said as she waved at Miguel. Me please said Michael. Oh, you are fuckin awake then are yer said Mary. Who fancies coming up to the old town for a bar crawl around the gay bars tonight? said Mary. All were in agreement. Can I dress up tonight Mary? said Gemma, if you like said Mary but make sure you look nice not like some tart. Why don't you and Mary come up to my suite early tonight Gemma we can have a glass of champagne before dinner and I'll help you get ready, I've got a few accessories you can borrow. That would be nice said Mary. Thank you so much said Gemma that's really nice of you. Think nothing of it said Dolly us girls must stick together bring a few outfits up to the suite and we'll help you choose something nice.

I suppose I'd better go and find a pharmacy said Gordon and get his lordship some Imodium; do you know where there is one? Yeah there's one down the road I'll pull my shorts on and I'll walk down with you. Gordon had filled him in on his relationship with Ben and the whole airport saga. He doesn't deserve you said Larry. I know he doesn't, but part of our relationship is based on him being the master and me the slave. I've never really got all that said Larry. You'd make a lovely master Larry said Gordon. Well I'll try anything once said Larry.

Later on, Gordon's phone pinged, and it was a text from Ben, can you pass my phone please Larry, Larry leant over him in bed and passed it to him. He's awake and wants me to bring him something to drink said Gordon. That's a shame said Larry I was just about to get my second wind. Christ your insatiable giggled Gordon. Now don't forget what I said, if you're stuck for something to do tonight, I'll meet you downstairs and we can go out for a bite to eat and go and have a drink in one of the gay bars in the old town. That's nice of you but I don't want to get in the way with your friends. The way he said it made Larry look up. Look I know they are a bit rough and ready, but they are a nice crowd once you get to know them. I'll take your word for that laughed Gordon. You deserve a good slap for saying that said Larry. You're getting the hang of it then I see smiled Gordon.

Ben was planning on going to dinner at the Sabor restaurant in Altea with Simon. Simon had told him, being crew we get to know where all the best restaurants are all over the world. Simon was quite grand thought Ben but then every British Airways steward he'd ever met was the same, well turned out and smart. He liked that. He said the food at the Sabor was legendary and that there were lots of great places to eat in Altea which was only 10 minutes in a taxi. He'd told Simon to book it and he'd work out how to get rid of Gordon. Just then Gordon came back into the bedroom with some mineral water, biscuits and a chicken sandwich he'd bought at a local store. He said hi how are you feeling. Terrible Said Ben. I've bought you some Imodium, come on take these. He poured Ben a glass of mineral water. Are you sure you don't want a doctor said Gordon? No, I'm fine it'll pass. Gordon was being nice and not stroppy, Ben was hoping to instigate a row, which was hard because Gordon was being kind. So, have you survived a whole day in Benidorm then? You've not been set upon by a gang of tattooed lager louts from up north then? No not yet said Gordon carefully. I've been laying out around the pool; it was quite nice really. Wow said Ben laughing you've actually been mixing with the peasants. I got talking to one or two people Gordon said they've asked me to join them for a drink and a bite to eat if you are not up to it. Are you going to be able to come out tonight? he asked Ben. No, I'm sorry, I'm really not up to it. Ben couldn't believe his luck this was going better then he could have imagined. Look if your serious about these people you've met, go with them. I don't expect you to stay in here with me. I'll watch a movie on my lap top I'm fine and I can order from room service if I want anything. Where are they taking you? Somewhere local they recommended a Spanish Paella restaurant up the road. That sounds lovely, go on, go and enjoy yourself. Ok I will, but I want to leave for Valencia tomorrow if your well enough. Ok deal said Ben. I'm just going to have a little siesta said Gordon do you need anything else. No, I'll try and go back to sleep too said Ben. Gordon texted Larry and said, looks like I'm free tonight if the offer is still open? Larry texted back. Yeah sure it is meet me in the bar downstairs at 7pm.XXxxx Gordon smiled and turned over. Ben was doing the same with Simon. Where shall we meet said Simon I'll come up to your room as soon as Gordon goes. Xxxxxx.

Yolanda was busy in the garden furnishing her yurts. She was making a very good job of it too. Can I come and look yet called out Roz from the kitchen door? No not yet wait till I tell you shouted Yolanda. She was busy arranging a welcome tray with herbal teabags and bottles of mineral water. Next to that was another tray with a selection of essential oils and oil burner and a packet of biodegradable wet wipes. She had decorated both the new yurt's identically, there were 4 beds, one double and two singles with a curtain that pulled around each bed, for privacy. Each bed had enough space next to it for a personal yoga mat. For bedside tables Yo had used upcycled wooden beer crates she had bought on Brighton market. There were candle lights, An LED torch, a recycled glass and a bottle of organic mineral water and tissues. There was a small bookcase containing feminist favourites like "Invisible women" (exposing data bias in a world designed for men) by Caroline Criado Perez, "Period Power (harness your hormones and get your cycle working for you) by Maisie Hill and Yo's personal choice of light reading "Honourable friends" by Caroline Lucas. The beds were not made up, but she had chosen some lovely bed sets, duvets stuffed with organic sheep's wool and ethically sourced organic cotton sheets and pillowcases. She had arranged fairy lights all around the top of the yurt's which were powered by the same solar panels that produced enough power for the cooking rings that were in the small kitchen area. They looked really pretty and Yo was pleased with herself, she sat alone for a minute in the circle in the middle between the beds she had left clear for chanting and mediation purposes. She breathed deeply for several minutes clearing her mind. Then she went out to get Roz who was now in the garage. They are ready if you want to come and have a look said Yo. Two minutes sweetheart I've just been knocking you up some of these out of these old skateboards of mine. What are they said Yo? Boot scrapers said Roz, you can put one outside each tent, I mean yurt, when the women come back from their walks, they can scrape their boots on them. Oh, Roz that's such a lovely idea thank you. Ah you're alright said Roz I don't want them jumping on those lovely sheets you've just bought with their boots on getting mud everywhere. Come on said Yo come and have a look I'm dying for you to see them.

Randy was taking the bandit boyz through their paces at the Sallis Benny theatre. Josh and Frank were sitting at the back watching them all. They were pleased. Frank said they are quite quick learners aren't they, yeah, I'm proud of them said Josh when Randy s through I want to get them singing and trying some of these moves. Randy had them all doing press ups, Right imagine you've got some beautiful guy laying underneath you or in your case Jack a skinny bird with huge tits. Jack tried hard not to laugh. Randy was watching these cute young men's buns going up and down and started feeling quite flushed. Right that's enough for now. Take 5 minutes and then Josh wants to try some of these moves with the song I hope you've all been learning? Ok Randy said Jack we all know it but it's a bit old isn't it? Well speak to Josh about that said Randy. Who the fuck is Sinitta anyway said Sam.? One of Simon Cowell's old fuck buddies said Harry. After the break Josh jumped up on stage and said right let's play this track through and let me see you use some of the moves you have learnt. Randy will guide you. Just for now try and lip sync if you can. He bent down and inserted an old Cd into the boom box he'd found in the cellar of the pub and Sinitta belted out "So many men so little time" A gay anthem from the 1980's. Frank sat at the back chuckling away. The boys looked a bit uncomfortable. Harry especially who looked a bit of a tough nut compared to the other two.

Cecil and Michael Were having a pre-dinner drink at Oscars bar around the corner from the Casa Don Phillipe hotel. They were sitting on the outside terrace with Alistair and Renaldo. So, did you two 'ave a quiet night last night then? said. Mike to Alistair. Yes, we did I'm afraid I needed it. I'm not used to all these late nights. We had a nice meal then bed with books said Renaldo very boring. Well I hope you're ready for tonight said Cecil after dinner there's a few of the late bars you haven't been to, yet we want you to see. Alistair laughed well ok ill last as long as I can.

Up in Dolly's suite, Dolly and Mary were putting the final touches to Gemma's wardrobe and make up. I see I'll have to take you shopping said Dolly looking at the selection of dresses Gemma had taken up to the suite. Still let's try and make the best of it. Here try this black dress on said Dolly. Mary helped Gemma get the dress over his head. Well I haven't got a bra that size, maybe we could do a bit of a job with some Sellotape. Take it off again. Dolly went into the bedroom and came back with some Sellotape she had bought to wrap up a few gifts for the others she was going to give them on the last night. Right push your boobs together Gem and hold them, not too much just give yourself a nice cleavage, that's it, now Mary you stand behind him and I'll pass the Sellotape to you around the back and we'll keep winding it round until it holds them up. Dolly went to the dressing table got out a blusher brush and applied some glitter blush to Gemma's cleavage. Right now, the face let's give you some eyebrows shall we said Dolly I'll do his nails said Mary. An hour later they were done. You've come up a treat said Mary. Dolly had made Gemma look pretty, she had redone the blonde wig Gemma had brought up with him a bit, so it looked more natural, less drag queen and with a good foundation, blusher and mascara Gemma had been transformed from Vikki Pollard to a pretty version of Gemma Collins. Mary went through some of Dolly's things and picked out a beautiful pink cashmere pashmina. Ere drape this around your shoulder's luv, Gemma looked in the mirror and felt himself welling up. Now don't fooking cry said Mary you'll ruin your make up. I don't know how to thank you two, you've turned me into what I've always wanted to be. Dolly went to the table in the sitting area and topped them all up with a glass of champagne. Cheers girls she said here's to a good night.

They went down and met the others in the bar. As they walked in Dolly and Mary stood back and let Gemma take centre stage. The other guys and one or two of the other customers burst into applause. Christ you look like Diana Dors said pissy Michael. Who's she said Gemma? A big film star of yesteryear dear said Michael. Oh, thanks said Gemma are you sure I look alright? You look bloody gorgeous said Tina Tits, if you don't pull someone tonight in that rig up,

I'll be damned said Harry. Where's Larry? said Mary, got a date said Michael despondently, who with? said Mary, that Gordon from Brighton, oh well good for him said Dolly come on let's go in and eat I'm starving.

They had one at the bar then went in for dinner. Afterwards Mary got two taxis organised outside the hotel and told the driver to take them all to GG's bar in the old town. She had said over dinner to Dolly and Gemma, some of these bars are men only but I've known most of the owners for years, so they let me in, but I'll tell 'em you two are both tranny's alright? Trans Mary Trans said Gemma oh for fooks sake Trans then said Mary. Do you think I'll pass? laughed Dolly. With that deep voice they won't even need to look under your skirt laughed Harry. Bloody cheek said Dolly. They all got into the taxis; Gemma got in the front with the driver who gave her the once over with very lustful eyes. Buenos noches senoras mi yama es Manolo. Gemma looked and fell in lust, he went bright red.

Larry had met Gordon in the bar earlier and they went out in search of somewhere to eat. I have got to be honest Larry there is nowhere around here I like the look of much. I mean I really don't want an all-day 5-euro breakfast, even with a pint of vodka and red bull thrown in. Do you fancy a walk said Larry? Sure, where do you have in mind. Well let's walk down onto the front and stroll up to the old town, there's lots of nice places up there to eat. Sounds great said Gordon. They crossed the road and made their way down onto the Levante beach, Gordon was quite startled. Oh, what a lovely beach he said. Oh yes, it's beautiful over a mile long too said Larry.

Ben and Simon were sat in the Sabor restaurant in Altea. Ben was impressed. Wow you have picked a great place Simon. Yes, it really is lovely I've been here loads of times and clock the waiters all of them look like models. Ben gazed around yes; I see what you mean taking in the tasteful trendy décor at the same time. Are you with anyone Simon at home I mean? asked Ben. No not at the moment. I've been flying solo for 2 years now if you'll forgive the pun. I'm not interested in a relationship at the moment, just after a good time. I want as much fun as I can get. What about you and Gordon? Oh, we are ok most of the time, we are both into S&M bondage etc, Simon looked up surprised really? Yes, we like Master and Slave, role play, orgies. Orgies? said Simon Yes, all that sort of thing said Ben. Do you fancy a bit of fun like that tonight, I know a great club with a big dark room at the back I could take you too? said Simon. Ben's face lit up, why not I could do with a bit of fun for a change. Just then Simons phone pinged, he looked at his phone. Shit, its work I've got to catch an afternoon flight tomorrow to Paris from Alicante. Better make the most of tonight then said Ben.

Alistair and Renaldo had finished their dinner at a fine dining restaurant in tapas alley they were walking back up to Oliver's to meet Cecil and Mike. Quite a crowd now had gathered on the outside terrace. Cecil shouted we've just paid us bill hang on we'll be with you. The four of them made their way around the three little streets that made up the gay village popping in each bar for a drink, much later on Michael said right now we will go to Peppermint. Not sure I can drink much more said Alistair. Have a few soft drinks like I do said Renaldo, they made their way to the peppermint bar, as they opened the door the extremely handsome Rene, the Dutch owners face lit up in a big smile and said welcome lads great to see you!

Mary had been welcomed by Luchie with lavish kisses on each cheek four times and a big hug. Mary darling so good to 'ave you back again. Ello Luchie luv I've got a few friends with me is it alright if I bring them in. Those two are trans whatsit said Mary there not real women luv is that alright? Sure, said Luchie am I not one myself he said fluttering his fan and eyelashes at the same time. Welcome to GG's all of you come in and have fun. Luchie looked at Dolly and said to Mary she's very good, muy bonito, she could pass anywhere. Mary laughed she paid him out of the whip money. Just pay for the others Mary I won't charge you, have a ticket with me. Oh, thanks darlin thanks very much said Mary. They got their drinks from the bar and made their way into the dance bar. Dolly Couldn't believe it. It's like something out of one of those old films. What dance is that said Gemma the pasodoble luv said Mary, never heard of it said Gemma. No, but your fanny was doing the pasodoble tonight when you saw that taxi driver though luv wasn't it. I saw you. I don't know what you're talking about laughed Gemma. Here look Mary look at pissy Michael said Gemma changing the subject. Mary looked over and nearly choked on her drink. Michael had died and gone to heaven he hadn't been sat down two minutes when this big German guy built like a brick shit house (as Mary would say) had asked Michael to dance. Without waiting for an answer, he pulled Michael onto his feet and was whisking him around the dance floor and then every now and then throwing him to the floor in a pasodoble "dip" Michaels glasses were a bit skew whiff but the smile on his face said it all.

Next up were Tina tits and Harry as soon as they heard the tango beat, they were up and whisking up and down very dramatically. Dolly and Mary were laughing until the tears ran down their faces. Dolly said in all my life Mary I have never seen anything so funny; fact is they are bloody good aren't they. Michael was sitting on the big Germans lap sipping a beer looking like a happy schoolgirl. I think he's pulled said Dolly. Just shows there is some one for everyone, there's hope for us yet Dol said Mary. Oh, bloody good luck to him, poor bugger let's just hope old Herman there is into fooking water sports. They both started laughing hysterically again. Gemma sat there looking very glamorous but was a bit bemused by it all. Mary told Dolly to go and have a look in the next room. Dolly stuck her head in and gasped as she saw two guys doing the 69 on the big screen. She went back to Mary, Mary was killing herself laughing, your face Dolly, oh you cow Mary fancy sending me in there, it's bigger than my local Odeon. After an hour or so the gang decided to make their way back into town to go to the peppermint bar. Now mind said Mary to Gemma and Dolly be careful, it's a nice bar but there's a dark room out the back where all sorts goes on so stick to the bar right? Harry and Tina said oh we might take a look, well you two can but Dolly and Gemma need to stick at the bar with me. Pissy Michael had fell in love and decided to go home with the German, so Mary said be careful luv any trouble ring my mobile. Michael walked off, oy! Mary yelled what said Michael? No barebacking do you hear me? Oh, dear god said Michael cringing with embarrassment.

So, the 5 of them walked down the hill and into the old town gay village, Mary went in first and Rene spotted her and came running out from behind the bar, hello love, how are you? so nice to see you again said Rene. He scooped Mary up in his arms and gave her a big kiss. Oh, Rene luv its lovely to see you again too darlin. These are my friends, all come in you are all welcome said Rene. As their eyes adjusted to the light, they spotted Alistair and Renaldo and Cecil and Michael at the bar. Lots of hellos and kisses and very quickly there was a round of drinks put in front of them. There was much hilarity and sending up and a good night was being had by all. At about 1 am the door opened and in walked Manolo the taxi driver, he ordered a drink and then spotted Gemma, he made his way straight over to him and said can I buy you a drink Senorita? Gemma blushed bright red and said I'm ok thanks. No, you're fookin' not you dozy cow said Mary let him buy you a drink. Ok Gemma turned to Manolo and said cheers I'll have a vodka tonic. My pleasure bonito said Manolo eyes full of lust. Mary eyed him up and down. He looked ok. About 40 a bit of a paunch but nice wavy hair and a nice smile. Big muscled arms, she'd keep an eye on the situation.

After Ben and Simon had finished dinner, they got a taxi back into Benidorm old town and started doing a round of the bars, Simon said if you are still feeling naughty, that bar I mentioned is just down there, Simon pointed. Ben said lead me to it. They walked down from Men's bar down to the peppermint they arrived half an hour before Mary and Co. They took their drinks and made their way into the dark room in Peppermint. When they got in there Simon found himself sharing the biggest dick he had ever had with another guy on his knees, Ben unzipped and stuck his into the mix and a couple of others from the back came forward. Soon it was in full swing, with every variety of sexual behaviour taking place.

Once Tina Tits and Harry Harrington had had a few more gin and tonics they said come on where on holiday we've got nothing to lose and slipped away from the others and went in the back to join in the orgy. Mary stayed with Dolly and the others from Brighton, Gemma was all loved up and snogging Manolo, Manolo said I want you, but I am married with children, you can come in my taxi with me to somewhere. When Gemma told Mary and Dolly, Dolly said no love, you're not doing that. Mary let Gemma take him back to your room, fook off said Mary. No let him do it you can come up and sleep in my suite with me there is a spare bed in the lounge area. Give him a chance for some happiness said Dolly. Oh, alright Mary said, Gemma you can have the room tonight but don't open the fooking safe whatever you do, all my jewellery and cash is in there. Oh, thanks Mary said Gemma you are such a love. He seems really nice; it makes a change for a man to fancy me as me and not a punter wanting me to pretend to be Divine or some other fat slob. Well just you be careful and make him wear a condom, no bare backing ok said Mary. I promise said Gemma. Soon he and Manolo were back in his taxi heading back for a night of lust at the Helios hotel.

Dolly and Mary were now getting very pissed and having a good laugh with Cecil Mike and the others. Dolly was really slurring now and said I think I'd better go home Mary, oh not yet love have one for the road shall we than well get a taxi back. Oh, go on then slurred Dolly, she had a black cocktail dress on, and the strap kept falling off her shoulder and the hair was starting to look a bit dishevelled. They were halfway through the one for the road when the door opened, Mary clocked it first it was the Police. Mary being quick witted dived straight into the ladies toilet and bolted herself in the lock up. Four big burly Guardia civil walked in the bar with guns in holsters attached to their belts. One of them went up to speak to Rene, Rene turned the music off and turned up the house lights. The Four Guardia civil marched through into the dark room where pandemonium had broken out. When the house lights had gone up after an initial scream from Gordon and Harry and a few what the fuck's there were much louder what the fucks. Ben looked down and realised he was fucking Gordon. Simon was being fucked by Larry. Gordon bent over was sucking off Harry Harington while Tina was on his knees noshing off two big Spanish guys in the corner. Ben was the first with what the fuck are you doing here to Gordon? Gordon started weeping the shock was too much. (He and Larry had been the first to arrive in the bar after a quick dinner tapas style in tapas alley, Larry knew of the bar and suggested a bit of fun. Gordon as usual was up for anything) Just then the police walked in and caught them all el flagrante. There was a lot of shouting from the police telling them all to get dressed. They were all being arrested for public indecency. As they cuffed them to each other Harry Harrington and Tina were in tears, as they marched them through the bar Dolly saws Tina and Harry and walked straight up to the first policeman and started yelling you can't arrest them, they are my friends they are English you bastards. So, they arrested her too and she was thrown into the back of the police wagon with all the rest of them and carted off to Benidorm Police station.

The police had asked all the other customers to leave the bar, so Alistair and Renaldo a bit scared and Cecil and Mike had legged it as soon as possible. They were walking quickly up the hill back to the Casa Don Phillipe, all shocked and burbling away. Oh, dear said Alistair I've never seen anything like it in my life. It was like one of those American films you see on the telly. Eye said Mike I've never seen owt like it neither. Mind you if the Benidorm Guardia are short of funds, they do start fining the bars. If you have one table extra on the terrace for instance said Cecil, they fine the bars a fortune, cash obviously, to fill the funds up for the firework extravaganza on new years' eve and the Benidorm festival in November. Fooking stunning they are too said Mike. But those poor bastards are going to have a rough night.

Back at the peppermint Mary had crept out of the toilet when she felt the coast was clear. Rene surprised laughed when he saw her. Oh, Mary you got away. Too right luv I hid in the fooking toilet, I know when the Guardia arrive anywhere its best to disappear. I've been coming here for years darlin. Don't worry love said Rene if they've got money it will all be sorted. Well I'm not sure about that said Mary. Forget it Mary they will ask me for a few hundred euros, and it will be forgotten have a brandy with me you look like you could do with it and me too actually. So, Rene poured them two very large Soberano brandies and they started to plan what to do.

Basically, you need to go to the police station in the morning with a credit card or cash said Rene. I haven't got enough luv not for that I'll have to message home to Josh and Frank and see if they can help, I'd better get back to the hotel luv, I can't even go to me own bed tonight luv I've let fat Gemma and that taxi driver have it, if there's any fooking stains on my sheets tomorrow they'll be hell to pay. Rene locked up the bar and walked Mary down to the taxi rank.

Meanwhile back at the police station in Benidorm, they had all been photographed and fingerprinted, Harry Harrington looked like he was in a coma with the shock. His wig was skew whiff and back to front which didn't look very good on the mug shots.

Dolly had sobered up quite quickly and said to Ben do something you're the lawyer and I'll try and use my experience to get us out of here. They took the men to a cell but left Dolly sitting in reception. She sauntered up to the desk sergeant equivalent and said in her deep voice I'd like to see whoever is in charge here please, I have a health condition which needs attending to, I'm diabetic 1 and I also suffer from claustrophobia. She opened her bag and slid 200 euros into the desk sergeants' hand. I'll see what I can do senora said the desk sergeant. Please said Dolly dramatically. Within 20 minutes she was called into to the duty inspectors office. The others were locked up in a communal cell with a load of Spanish street people it was hell. Ben knowing a few things about European law demanded a phone call and told them he was an English abogado (lawyer). They realised he meant business and let him out to make a call, the others sat very tightly together trembling and saying oh god I wish I were at home in England in bed.

Dolly was shown into the head chiefs office, she had rechecked her hair in a trip to the ladies and was ready for business. She noticed that Inspector Martinez couldn't take his eyes off her breasts. They were sticking out over the top of the cocktail dress. She was channelling Marilyn. She sat down crossing her legs slowly. Now inspector my friends and I are on holiday and there seems to be a little bit of a mistake. Yes, they have been silly boys, but they are on holiday and a bit drunk, what is its going to cost us to get out of here without going to court? Inspector Martinez could not take his eyes off of Dolly's tits. Knowing this she rubbed a hand over them dropped her shoulder straps and pushed her breasts over the top of the black cocktail dress. She started playing with her nipples and licking her lips. For a gal in her 60's she was doing a great job. Inspector Martinez gasped in wonder and under his desk unzipped his flies and put his right hand to work. In 5 minutes, it was all over. Dolly walked up to the desk and handed Inspector Martinez a tissue. Now then how much to get my two friends out? 500 euros each in cash said Inspector Martinez. Dolly opened her bag whacked a grand on the table and said right tell your boys to let them out I want Terry Malone and Harry Harrington. What you do with the rest is up to you. Fair exchange plus these said Dolly running her hand over her breasts and down her front. Si said Inspector Martinez, you are beautiful. He pushed the intercom and called for Tina and Harrys release. Dolly met them out front and they ran up to her like a mother and cried on her shoulder. Right you two hold it together and walk out of here with your head held high, follow me. She glided out of the police station giving a little wave and a nod and a smile en route as they reached the exit, she flagged a taxi. Right come on boys all back to the hotel up to my suite for a large brandy each get over it and then go to bed. I don't know how to thank you said Tina, don't worry you can pay me back weekly said Dolly. Harry said I'll pay you back right now and I'll never be able to thank you enough. Its ok Harry pay me back when we get home, I've had a lot of experience of police stations over the years with my old man I know how it works.

When they got back to the hotel they got up to Dolly's suite and found Mary passed out fully clothed clutching her handbag to her chest. Wake her up gently Harry while I pour us a brandy. When Mary came to, she gasped and said what the fuck are you doing here? Dolly got us out said Tina she's been our saviour said Harry. How said Mary, Dolly pushed her breasts together and winked, no way said Mary you didn't give someone a tit wank did you? No, I didn't said Dolly laughing but I got them out, I could tell he was a tit man, he had a wank under the desk it was all over in 5 minutes. I put a grand down for the boys and we were out. My mother and Fred always said always make sure you've got plenty of cash on you and I always have. Fooking ell said Mary I couldn't have done that. Well let's be honest Mary said Dolly you haven't got these have you? She said pushing her cleavage together. They all burst out laughing.

Underneath down in Marys room. Gemma had fallen in love. Manolo had been honest. He wasn't gay but he found transvestites very sexy. He made love to Gemma 3 times during the night, with such gentleness and with so much passion too, Gemma had tears running down his face. Why are you crying said Manolo, am I hurting you? Hurting me? said Gemma god no, thank you for loving me. Manolo gently kissed away his tears. He stayed until 6 am and made arrangements to come back later in the day and take Gemma out for a few hours in the afternoon to a deserted farmhouse on the edge of Finestrat village. It had belonged to his grandmother. His wife didn't want to live in it, preferring one of the more modern town houses they had built in nearby La Nucia.

Ben once he had got his head around the situation had gone into full human rights lawyer mode, demanded an interpreter and already boned up on EU law he was able to quote tooth and nail legalities to the Spanish police. They had no choice but to let them out, they had done nothing wrong. So, he Gordon, Simon and Larry were let out with the two Spanish guys at 5am. The four of them went back in the taxi in silence and went to their rooms.

Ben said to Gordon just go to bed we will talk tomorrow. Gordon did as he was told.

Thursday

Ollie was typing away at his desk in his home office he was progressing very well with the restaurant branding job. Will was downstairs in the garage/ therapy room with a client. This wasn't a happy ending affair although Will rather wished it was. It was a sports massage for one of the footballers from the Brighton Albion team. A handsome player with thighs to die for. Will had been treating a muscle

147

strain injury in his leg for a few weeks now, and the player was really impressed and said he would recommend his team mates to come to Will. They had plenty of masseuses at the club but being right on the outskirts of town it could be difficult to get there with the traffic, so sometimes it made sense to go local. After all footballers could afford it. He always gave Will a £20 tip on top of the fee price.

John when he finished work was sitting with his feet up as was Grant just chilling watching TV, John had his laptop on his lap and had plugged in the memory stick containing the files with Paul Bryans sex videos on. He had the sound down but what he was seeing was sensational. The MP in all sorts of get ups and positions with various celebrities and famous politicians. One included and orgy with several well known people in the same room together, he started to tell Grant, but Grant wasn't having it. I don't want to know John thanks. What your doing is dangerous. John kept shtum but he was already spending the money he knew he was going to get from the newspapers for these revelations.

Josh was on his way round to the Sallis Benny theatre to go through the song and routine with the boys. He wanted them now to sing live and dance at the same time. The boys said they had been practising at home at every opportunity they had. Josh believed them; they were a nice bunch of lads. Randy was there to guide, after about the 10th attempt, they had it off pat. Sinitta's old song 'so many men so little time' had been transformed with a rap section in the middle. It was upbeat, funny and catchy.

Well done lads 1 down 7 more to go, groans from the lads, but smiles too. They were loving it. Josh wanted

8 numbers in the act so he could start booking them into club dates around the country to gain experience.

The Royal Sisters were in their summer house where Karl was fitting Kristabelle for one of his outfits for the summer ball. Yards of red sequined fabric laid on the floor. Oh, I'm so excited said Kris, I'm going to look amazing. I think I'll have to pad you out a bit said Karl you're are far too thin. I think you need to go back to the doctor love and have a word about it. Kris sighed, I know you are right, he could never lie to Karl. He had been throwing up more than usual lately, his bulimia had come back with a vengeance.

Mary, Dolly and the others were all late down to the pool, the next morning. They were all a bit quieter than normal. Gemma came down with a big smile on his face, unaware of the dramas the others had had, he was in love. Manolo was coming back to the hotel at two o'clock to pick him up and go up to granny's old finca in Finestrat.

The rest of the holiday went along just fine with no major dramas. They stuck to bars without dark rooms though and had a good laugh at the Casa Don Phillipe playing "Play your cards right" with the Duchess, they even had a couple of beach days where they played cards and kept giggling over the events. Pissy Michael went out for the days and most nights with Herman the German. Gemma came back and packed a few things and moved into Granny's Finca for a few days. A pretty little country farmhouse. Gemma had his hair in a scarf daytimes sweeping away cobwebs and polishing grannies old furniture turning it into a real little love nest for himself and Manolo. He was dreading Monday coming when he would have to leave.

Ben and Gordon had woken early and had a deep discussion about their relationship, it was decided that Gordon could introduce Larry as an alternative master into the relationship during orgies or on nights he wanted to spend with Simon. It was not easy, but they decided it was the grown-up way to go forwards. Ben also explained that he would need to spend more time in London and around the country as there was an extremely lucrative bit of business developing at an alarming rate for human rights lawyers. Mainly the economic migrants coming over in dinghies from France who were claiming asylum. The government working with various companies were paying to put these illegal immigrants and a few genuine asylum seekers up in hotels paid for by the British taxpayers until they could deport the ones that were not genuine asylum seekers. It was Ben and his friends' job along with certain contacts at the home office to block the government at every turn so that these people could remain in the country indefinitely. Paid for using legal aid, Ben was mentally rubbing his hands together thinking of all the extra moolar. Their taxi pulled up outside the Hotel Helios and swept them off to grander destinations in Valencia.

Sunday

Last day for Cecil Michael Alistair and Renaldo

Saturday night had been a repeat of the week before

plus they had gone back into town after GG's and visited all the bars, and the people they had made friends with over the trip to say goodbye. They didn't get to bed until 4am.

The next morning, they were all hungover and Renaldo groaned while he packed his case. Alistair said I wish I could get straight on that plane and fly straight back to my bed in Queens Crescent. Well you can't said Renaldo the flight isn't until 8pm tonight, we have to check out at 12pm, we've got the rest of the day to kill. After a couple of Coffees in the bar with Cecil and Mike who were also suffering a bit, they were feeling a bit more human. I'm glad we booked the return flight from Alicante said Renaldo I don't fancy that drive through Valencia today. They all decided to get a cab and go together to pick the car up, they were all booked on the same flight home. If you like we can have a little drive in the country today, clear the cobwebs said Renaldo. Great idea said Mike if you don't mind us tagging along again, not at all said Renaldo. You can leave your handbags and suitcases here my loves said the Duchess I'll lock them up in the cellar. Come back later for them when you're ready to go to the airport. Thanks, my love said Cecil.

They picked up the car and took a drive up to the beautiful picturesque village of Finestrat, then they drove across a very windy country road with a few hair pin bends that had Cecil hanging on in the back with gritted teeth. Slow down Renaldo said Alistair. Don't worry I know these roads like the back of my head said Renaldo. Hand said Alistair. They drove through a town called La Nucia up into another little stunning village called Polop where they parked up

and went for a livener. They found a pretty bar in the
Square called La Font. They sat down at a table
outside. What a charming village said Alistair, yes
and there's a few friends of Dorothy's up here as well
said Mike gazing at the table opposite where a good-
looking Scotsman was holding court, to a small group
of gay men. They had a cold beer each and then
decided to drive down to Altea for lunch. A toast,
said Alistair once they had got a seat at the Sabor
restaurant in the harbour, to good friends, good health
and may we all return soon to this beautiful place. I'll
drink to that said Mike. Cheers.

They said a tearful farewell to the Duchess and had a
no hassle journey back to Brighton where they
dumped the cases in their hallways and went straight
to bed.

Monday

Mary made sure they were all up and down to
breakfast. Cases packed they left them in the room
behind reception while they went in for breakfast.

Gemma packed his things with tears pouring down
his face. Stay said Manolo you can live here as my
other wife. Please bonito I implore you. I can't said
Gemma I have to go back; I just can't stay here with
no money or a job. Plus, I can't let my bosses down,
they've been so good to me. Also, my landlady she
relies on my rent, and all my stuff is in England.
Manolo sat with his head in his hands on the bed in
despair.

Eventually they all made their way to Alicante
Airport including a weeping Gemma and a very

subdued pissy Michael. After checking in they headed straight for the bar and Dolly ordered everyone drinks. They had quite a few before boarding. The party carried on, on the plane home and by the time the minibus pulled up outside the Fawcett Inn, they were feeling no pain. They piled into the bar with a big cheer going up from the regulars. Josh ran around from the bar and hugged Mary and Dolly, we've really missed you all, did you have a great time? You'll never fooking believe it dear said Mary, get us all a drink Josh and we'll tell you what happened luv.

Brighton's Got Talent Finale. Sunday July 7th

Over two months had passed since Easter. Summer had arrived and it was very hot in Brighton. Today would mark the day when the 6 finalists for the Brighton's got talent show would compete for the top places. After weeks of auditions and try outs only three lucky ones would win, and the winner would get a chance to appear alongside Daisy Froglette in the entertainment tent at Brighton Pride which was always held on the first Saturday in August. The Fawcett Inn was heaving. They had all the doors and windows open, but it was still like a sweat box. Lunch had been served but Gemma was only offering sandwiches and salads as it was too hot to cook roasts. By 4.30pm you couldn't move in the pub. Everyone waiting for 5 o'clock for the big finale.

At 10 to Five Frank put on the show tune

introduction and then with the stage lights on he brought on Daisy Froglette to serious applause and cheers. Daisy took to her throne and said Frank is going to explain how to vote for the person or persons who you want to win. Its technology that doesn't register with my old brain my dears, so I'll hand you back to Frank. Frank took the mike and started to explain.

For those of you who don't already know we have designed an app for the pub, I want those of you who haven't already done so to download it to your phones now. Just type in The Fawcett Inn into google play or the apple shop. On there you will see a picture and the name of the 6 acts in tonight's show. In the first round I want you to vote for who you would like to see in the final 3 by clicking on their name or photo so you can each vote for 3 acts in the first round ok? Then in the second round after an interval. I want you to vote for who you want to be the winner of the 2018 Brighton's got talent. Has everybody got that? Yes, came the reply. Good, for anyone who is elderly or doesn't have a smart phone there are voting forms all around the bar, just fill them in and post in the box either side of the bar and Mary and Olly will count them in the interval and at the end. Ok Ill hand you back over to the wonderful Miss Daisy Froglette, John Bishon played the intro and Daisy was off, having a change opened with 'another opening another show' one of his old standards from years ago. Then with a big drum roll the talent show began.

First up in no particular order, (the contestants had pulled a number out of the hat) Was Lauren Anderson the fabulous singer with a voice like Adele.

She sang 'Someone like you' to rapturous applause and bravo's, think we've got a bit of competition with her said Josh quietly to Frank. We'll see said Frank. Next up was Sandy Lane the drag comic. He opened with a song then did 6 minutes stand up which went down well with most of the crowd, he was a little bit un PC and swore quite a bit so some of the more woke types in the audience were a bit po faced. Then it was time for Toto and Dorothy the dog act. This went down a bomb, it was high camp mixed with some really good tricks that toto was able to perform, with lots of clips edited together from the soundtrack of the wizard of oz to add to the fun. At the end Dorothy clutching Toto span around at quite a speed for a big hairy bear, to the tornado scene in Oz, he finished with the immortal line looking around the crowd said. Toto, "I don't think we are in Kansas anymore" Huge applause and bravos. The Bandit boys were next, and they bought the house down with 'So many men so little time' People were standing on chairs and craning their necks to see the boys dancing around shirtless just in tight jogging pants and trainers. Lots of hearts were a flutter in the audience. They were hot and they knew it. Randy had showed them how to work the crowd and they were lapping it up. Johnny Reynolds was next the 19-year-old singer. He did a cover version of Cher's "Believe" again to tremendous applause he had a great voice. This is going to be a tough one to call luv Mary said to Olly, both behind the bar and serving and watching at the same time. The talent this year is incredible said Olly really top notch. They are all good. Dolly sitting at the bar dressed head to toe in vintage Christian Dior said to Mary you're right I couldn't pick a winner, but I really like Lauren and the bandit boyz. Last up was Adam Assmaster the builder/stripper from Peacehaven. He had put together a new act which included fire eating. Frank was shitting himself standing by with a fire extinguisher. It was a great little act with lots of sexual titillation, instead of a member of the audience, he had dragged Johnny Reynolds from backstage to help him remove his G string. He'd worked himself up before going on and had put two tight elastic bands around the base of his knob to keep it hard. When Johnny pulled the g string away there were gasps from the audience Harry and Tina sitting in the front were fixated. Alistair was embarrassed, Renaldo was giggling. Mike and Cecil were laughing at Tina and Harry. Ben was with Steve and Gordon had his hand in Larry's and whispered in his ear, it's not as big as yours sir.

So that was it, Daisy asked them all to place their votes and called for an interval of half an hour. Voting would close in five minutes and all paper votes had to be placed in the boxes in 5 minutes when Frank and Olly would carry them out to the kitchen to be counted with Mary. Josh and Will were behind the bar and Dolly seeing them struggle with the crowds Jumped behind and gave them a hand serving. You never forget said Dolly, it's like riding a bike darling.

Olly was checking the app to see how many votes had been cast for who, then wrote it down, then he helped Mary with the paper votes. Frank and Josh said we don't want anything to do with it, everyone knows we are managing the boyz and we don't want to be accused of fiddling or anything. Let it be a fair contest anyway. Once the votes were counted and checked the answer was put in a sealed envelope which Mary handed to Daisy to open on stage. John Bishon struck up a few bars of 'Showbiz'as Daisy made his way back onto the stage. A huge drum roll came from Johns Synthesizer and Daisy said right shh everyone the results are in. He opened the envelopes. Glancing backstage at the contestants he said don't worry I won't drag out the agony like they do on TV.

So, The Three acts that have made it into the Final in no particular order are, Toto and Dorothy, a big cheer went up as Dorothy and Toto came onto the stage. Blimey said Frank to Josh didn't think that would be in the top 3, just shows you doesn't it said Josh chewing his nails with nerves. The Bandit Boyz, a huge cheer went up again with lots of wolf whistles as they boyz returned thank fuck for that said Josh. And finally, Lauren Anderson said Daisy. Again, big cheers from the crowd. This is going to be really close said Josh to Mary. Yes luv, I couldn't call it either, mind you I thought the stripper would get through seeing's how most of those in here love a bit of dick dear. Josh just laughed Mary didn't realise she was being funny because she was actually being serious. So now the three acts had to perform another number or skit they had rehearsed. Lauren did 'my one and only' by Adelle and a few people were in tears. Toto and Dorothy sat in a rocking chair miming to Judy Garland singing "over the Rainbow" before disappearing up the yellow brick road and the Bandit boys came on in Tight ripped designer jeans bare foot with tight white shirts opened to their navels and sang a stirring version of George Michael and Elton John's version of 'Don't let the sun go down on me'. Harry taking lead vocal as he was the best singer of the three. Frank and Josh looked on in pride as they lifted

157

the roof. The crowd loved it. The other contestants gave them a huge round of applause as they came off. There was lots of backslapping backstage and Daisy sat watching them with a smile on his face. Admiring their youthful energy their passion and their sense of fun. He remembered his ambition his dream to make it big when he was working in the kitchens at Claridge's in London as a young lad washing dishes, landing as a raw youthful 17 year old from a little village called Beer in Dorset he dreamt all day of how he would make it onto a stage to perform.

The Royal Sisters had crept in for the finale and they decided there and then to book Lauren Anderson and the Bandit boyz for the summer ball coming up now in two weeks' time.

The voting had been done and the count been completed, once again Daisy was handed the sealed envelope. A drum Roll and calls for silence.

In third place in Brighton's got talent 2018 is…….. a little pause. Toto and Dorothy. A big cheer went up Dorothy went on to collect his prize. In Second place its Lauren Anderson, again big cheers the votes for the top two had been very close. Lauren accepted her £500 with a big smile and thank you to the audience. So that means the winners are The Bandit Boyz. Yes, yelled Josh as he and Frank punched the air. The three cheeky Monkeys came on and the place went wild. Golden confetti fell from the roof as Frank pulled a cable to shower them all in a little gold dust. The Boyz were so excited and couldn't stop laughing and crying at the same time. They now had to reprise one of their numbers and they chose 'so many men' because it was upbeat and happy, the whole pub were up and dancing on the tables and chairs, everywhere.

The atmosphere was electric Mary turned to Josh and Frank and said in all my years here, I've never seen anything fooking like it dear never. Fooking marvellous. Josh and Frank leant down and kissed Mary then they picked her up and sat her on the bar. She couldn't stop laughing. Dolly still serving said enjoy yourself Mary you've earnt it darling.

It was only two weeks now until the summer ball, arrangements were well underway. Everyone in the Crescent and the 200 invited guest were getting their costumes ready, there was much excitement as this was becoming a Brighton highlight, a prequal to Pride in August.

Monday the 8th of July

Alistair had asked Gordon to pop around for a chat at 11 am that morning and a coffee. Gordon was at work but slipped out for half an hour. Hey guys, he said as Alistair and Renaldo opened the door together. Come in please said Alistair. They sat down together, and Alistair said. Gordon, we have decided to move to Valencia. Really said Gordon how lovely we had a great few day there. What brought that on? Well when we were there recently, I realised how much Renaldo misses his family. He really isn't happy here anymore. Oh, I wouldn't say that said Renaldo interrupting. Well not as happy said Alistair, also I really fell in love with the area, I even enjoyed Benidorm great fun. Gordons stomach churned at the memory. I'm not getting any younger I think I would like to retire in the sun. I get on very well with Renaldo's family and it will be company for me too.

So, we were wondering if you would value the house for us. Sure, thing said Gordon. He had never been inside no 5 before despite living next door. Shall we do the tour? Renaldo showed him around and Gordon being Gordon tutted at some of the décor, said this bathroom is looking a bit tired, those fitted wardrobes need to go. All negative apart from you have a lovely garden. With a spruced up kitchen, I may be able to get you 500k tops. Is that all said Alistair? we paid 475k 3 years ago. Yes, well they were brand new then. Property is going up a bit but not at the rate it was in 2016, it's a buyers' market. They discussed terms and conditions. Alistair said he'd think about it. He had another estate agent coming around at 1 o'clock from Mission Accomplished's main rival Wolf and Sons. He'd see what they had to say. After Gordon left Renaldo said I don't like that man he did nothing but sneer when I showed him around. Such a snob. Don't let him have the business Alistair. I think you are right said Alistair. Why would he look down his nose at us? We are better educated have more money, so he doesn't like the curtains, so fuck him said Alistair. Renaldo startled said Alistair I've never heard you use that word before, well just occasionally it's the only Anglo Saxon word that's appropriate and they both laughed.

At one o'clock. The doorbell rang again, and it was Angela Major from Wolf and Sons. Hello, she said with a big smile, hand out thrust for a firm handshake. The first thing she said was oh what a lovely home you have here guys. And the garden is spectacular. Renaldo showed her around upstairs, good you've got wardrobes in the bedrooms always popular, really nice. They sat down and she said I think I could get you around 595-625 thousand for this property. I can gct a for salc board up tomorrow and a photographer around in the morning to do the outside and inside shots if that is convenient. The rate was 0.5 % lower than Gordon had quoted so the deal was struck.

Gordon got straight on his mobile to Ben after he had been in to no 5 and said. You'll never guess what, Alistair and Renaldo are moving to Valencia. They've just asked me to come and do a valuation for them. Really? said Ben, what's it like? Well a bit old fashioned but that's just the furniture really a lick of paint and a good clean up should do it said Gordon. Well for god sake go through your client list straight away and select a group to view. We don't want any undesirables moving in next door. Don't worry I put a cross next to our gay client's names, so they get priority said Gordon. Yes, well pick someone nice to live there then said Ben firmly. Yes sir of course I will sir. Good boy now get to work.

So, there was much consternation in the Crescent when they all saw the for sale board go up at no 5. Alistair popped over to tell Cecil and Mike their plans, and they could not have been happier for them. Good luck to you both said Mike you only live once go for it and we'll be able to see you a couple of times a year when we come over to Beni. They all had a hug. We shall miss you though said Cecil, really, you've been lovely friends to us not like your stuck up neighbours.

Yo saw it on her way back from school, she said have you seen the for sale sign up outside no 5? to Roz. Yeah, I saw it, think they are moving to Spain or something. Oh well I hope we get someone decent move in there said Yo anxiously, what do you mean by decent? asked Roz. Well hopefully someone gay, preferably a woman and definitely not a bloody Tory said Yo shuddering. That's not very diverse is it love said Roz smiling. Yo left the room sharpish and went to put the kettle on.

Most of the others wished the guys luck. The only other two having a little bitch were the Royal Sisters. Fancy moving abroad at his age, I wouldn't fancy it dear said Kris, Well neither would I what about healthcare? After Brexit there won't be any of that will there said Kris. Well maybe if they get married Alistair will qualify. Which is exactly what Alistair and Renaldo planned to do but in Spain with all the family in attendance.

And it seems Alistair and Renaldo were not the only ones on the move. Gemma was sitting in Josh and Franks office at the pub. I'm sorry to tell you this guy's but I'm going to leave. Why said Josh crestfallen. I'm going to move to Spain said Gemma. Really said Frank. Yes, I met a lovely man over there at Easter called Manolo. He's married with kids, but his wife is a strict catholic and doesn't want any more babies, so she has said no more sex! and I know he loves me. He's setting me up in his late granny's country house. A finca they call it. It's a nice little place, needs modernising a bit but it's quiet and rural and I can keep a few pets there. I'll be happy. We have facetimed each other every single day since I got back, and I know he's the one. He's only a taxi driver and he's got a family to support but he's lined me up a job working on his much older brothers farm further up the hill a bit. He keeps goats and needs someone to milk them, plus he needs someone to cook and clean for him. Apparently, he has quite a bit of dosh stashed away and he's willing to pay me a reasonable wage, well enough to live on anyway. He thinks I'm a woman, so I'll have to dress permanently now in women's clothes, but that suits me, I feel more comfortable like that anyway. The electricity comes from a generator so no bill. The heating is a log burner and they deliver gas bottles to cook with, so I'll have very little outgoings. and Manolo has promised to buy me a new TV and get Wi-Fi installed so I can stay in touch with you all.

Well aren't you full of surprises eh? Said Josh smiling. I think its lovely. Me too said Frank, when are you going? Well I'll give you a months' notice said Gemma. That's great said Josh all though I'm sorry you are going. I am too said Gemma and it wasn't an easy decision, especially to leave Wendy, she cried for hours after I told her. Poor Wendy said Frank. Yes, but take a look at me guys, I'm a joke in this town, I still get the piss taken out of me near where I live by the local kids. I've had it every day since I was a child. This is my one chance of happiness. I can't believe he finds me attractive, but he does. So, I've got to go for it. Of course, you have said Josh getting up behind the desk and giving Gemma a big hug. We wish you all the happiness in the world said Frank. When Gemma told Mary, she went very quiet and walked to the ladies and had a good cry. Gemma had become like a daughter to her. She pulled herself together, dried her eyes put her big framed glasses back on and walked out of the toilet with a smile on her face. She went into the kitchen and threw her arms around Gemma, I wish you all the luck in the world darlin I really do, thanks Mary said Gemma I'll see you when you come out on holidays. You will said Mary and I'll tell you another thing, if that cont starts mistreating you or knocking you about or owt you get on the phone to me, and me and Dolly will be straight out on the next flight and we'll bash is fooking brains out. Right? Right said Gemma. What do you fancy for lunch Mary? Have you got any of those fresh prawns left said Mary? Yes still a few in the fridge their ok still fresh. I'll have a bowl of them with some vinegar and black pepper and a slice of bread and butter please luv said Mary heading out to open up the bar.

Tuesday 9 of July

John and Grant had finished all the work at MP Paul Bryans house in Hove and were having a rest between jobs. He was sat in the kitchen at the island on a stool with his laptop, copying a few bits of the video clips he had of Paul Bryan in compromising positions with well known people. He had already contacted the editors of several red top daily newspapers, who were more than interested. He had meetings up in London with one of the big guys on Thursday. He was due to take the kids out for the evening after school for a meal, so Grant didn't suspect anything.

Ben had arranged to meet Gordon for dinner at Browns restaurant in Duke street Brighton after work. After a nice meal in the established restaurant and a bottle of good claret, they walked around to the taxi rank in the Steine and headed home. When the taxi pulled up outside their house, they both saw at the same time the for sale sign outside Alistair and Renaldo's house. What the fuck said Gordon angrily. They got out of the taxi and starred. I thought you said you had it all sewn up said Ben, I did said Gordon I'm not having this. With that Gordon stormed up the drive and rang the bell. Both Alistair and Renaldo came to the door. Good evening can we help you said Alistair. What the fuck is that sign doing there said Gordon? Ben stood at the gate listening. It's a for sale board said Renaldo. I can see that but why? you agreed to let me handle the sale. I agreed to no such thing said Alistair. I gave you first chance at it, but after your sneering, patronising attitude and the fact that you undervalued our property I decided to let Wolf and Sons handle the sale and marketing. But they might sell to anybody! said Gordon. Good that's their job said Alistair, goodnight and slammed the door in Gordons face. Ben listening at the bottom of the drive was seething. As Gordon walked back down, he said get in that house now. When they got in Ben turned nasty. You absolute fucking idiot said Ben, turned your nose up at them did you, you fucking hateful little snob. Before Gordon had time to answer Ben reached back and slapped his face with his great big hand and with such force it sent Gordon flying into the hall table which collapsed under the weight. But Ben hadn't finished as he walked past, he kicked Gordon hard in the stomach and shouted sometimes I hate you, you ridiculous cunt. Go and sleep in the dungeon and lock the door. I won't be held responsible for what I might do if you don't get out of my face right now. Gordon whimpered and scared crawled up two flights of stairs and did as he was told. Ben poured a large scotch, reached into the kitchen draw and got out a bag of Charlie. He had four lines before he could calm down.

Pissy Michael walked into the Fawcett Inn dead on 6'oclock ready for his evening session. There was a gasp from the others When Herman the German walked in behind him, Fucking Nora said Mary, you can say that again said Dolly. Look who's come to see me said Michael. We can see dear said Tina tits. Everybody this is Ralph who I met on holiday. I thought his name was Herman said Larry to Dolly, just a nickname darling. Dolly was first to offer her hand. Welcome Ralph nice to see you again, how are you? Let me get you a drink and one for Michael please Mary. A beer please said Ralph and Michael had a gin and tonic. The others said hello and made friendly gestures. They all moved up a bit so they could both sit at the bar with them.

So, when did all this happen then said Mary? We've been emailing each other since I got back said Michael, he's retired like me, so I've invited him over to stay for a month and see how it goes. Bloody hell said Mary you quiet ones are the worst. Well cheers to you both said Dolly I hope you have a lovely stay Ralph. Cheers to you all said Ralph. Does he know about your problem said Mary out of the corner of her mouth? Yes, he does, he used to be a senior nurse on a psychiatric wing, so he says a little bit of wee doesn't upset him. Plus, he's going to teach me some techniques to try and control it. If not, he knows a doctor in Germany who might be able to correct the problem with a little operation. Great said Mary, why have you never let the NHS sort it out. My doctor said it was just my age said Michael. Oh well good luck to you darlin' said Mary.

John was on the 8.20 am Brighton to Victoria train he had arranged to meet this editor in the Grosvenor Hotel which was attached to Victoria station. A nice quite grand 4 star hotel. The editor had hired a suite for the day so they could work out a deal. Johns London lawyer Marc Johnson was meeting him off the train, an old friend from way back he was shit hot and dealt with some of London's more shady characters and was used to working out lucrative expose deals like this one. John had had several newspaper's bidding for the story after he had telephoned several. He sent a few still pictures via email and let the bidding begin. He settled on The Moon a red top rag with a huge readership and their sister Sunday paper the "Sunday World News" When he arrived at reception, he was given directions to the editor's suite. He rang on the door. When it was opened there was the famous Kevin Reagan, one of the most famous editors and journalists in fleet street sitting on a sofa plus two lawyers and his private secretary Anna who said pleased to meet you John. Marc Johnson said Johns lawyer extending a hand. Pleased to meet you said Anna John had not given them his surname or address. She led them into the room and introduced him to the others. Kevin said have you brought the whole film with you? Yep said John it's all on a memory stick in my pocket tapping

167

his jeans front right hand side. So, let's talk money said John. Well I'd like to see the film first said Kevin, yes, I bet you would laughed John keeping it light, but I want to see the contract your guys over there have knocked up, I want complete anonymity. Payment made into my lawyers account with so much in cash or put into a trust fund for my two kids. How much did you have in mind? John looked him straight in the eye and said, one million pounds sterling without blinking. Kevin roared with laughter, yes, I bet you do. It's worth it said John. What I've got on here is dynamite. The haggling and arguing went on, they eventually agreed £750.00 for the serialisation and the book rights. £500.000 paid into a protected account held by Marc Johnson until needed and £250.00 put into a trust fund arranged again by Marc Johnson for Johns two children. The lawyers drew up the contracts. Kevin and John both signed them. It was agreed the Lawyers and Marc Johnson would hold the contracts until they had all seen the film, if Kevin was satisfied with what he saw. The lawyers would hand over the contracts and the money would be arranged by electronic transfers.

John inserted the memory stick into the smart tv on the wall and the fun began. John stood all the way through just by the tv protecting the memory stick. There was much hilarity and swearing from Kevin as the film progressed. Fuck me not him as well said Kevin as a previous Primeminister was caught bending over a sofa and being fucked hard by a black rent boy. It went on and on. When the clip changed to the one where Paul Bryan was on his knees giving the prominent member of the house of commons Walter Burke a blow job. Kevin was hysterical he kept yelling Order! Order! and killing himself laughing. When it finished. Kevin said well I don't know where you got this from, but this is the hottest story to break since the Cyril Smith scandal. It will rock the nation. He told Anna to open the bar and champagne flowed for a good hour. The deal was completed.

Once the money had been transferred John handed over the memory stick and shook hands With Kevin Reagan. Kevin said that story was worth a million, probably 2 million. John was happy though, he was only expecting a couple of grand, he'd just used his street boy instincts and gone in at the top. Now he had enough to pay off his and Grants mortgage and put some money away for his children for when they were older. Job done.

The Summer Ball Saturday July 28th, 2018

So, the big day had eventually arrived. The grand marquee had been erected on the green for three days now and took over three quarters of the space. The back of the marquee was facing the summer house/tearoom which was cleverly being used as a dressing room for the acts that would appear. The stage had been built at the back so the acts could run backstage down a few steps and out into the summer house to change and rest.

Inside the marquee in front of the stage there was a good size dance floor. Around the dance floor and towards the entrance about halfway were 20 tables each seating ten people, covered with the best white starched linen cloths scattered with diamante crystals and elaborate candelabras that were lit with led light bulbs. Real candles were out much to Kris's disgust because of health and safety laws. There was no cutlery as the only food being circulated were trays of canapés. However, each table contained 10 beautiful wine glasses, starched linen napkins and two ice buckets each with a selection of chilled white and rose wines. Other drinks were available at the bar, but they had to be paid for. The other residents had refused to contribute more than they usually contributed towards the event, so the balance had to be made up with Karl's savings. It was quite a lot, so they had decided to hold a raffle and had got friends with (or associated with) local businesses to donate prizes, A night at the Grand hotel, A weekend for two at Hero's hotel, theatre tickets for west end shows. Nice prizes and they hoped that the sale of these items at £10 a strip would go a good way towards covering the costs, if not all of them. The catering company had provided a long elegant bar, and Josh and Frank had set it up with draught beer pumps, spirits and mixers. So as the guests came in, they would find the elegant bar on the right serviced by Olly, Will and Josh all wearing crisp well ironed white shirts with black bow ties and black waistcoats and black trousers. Karl had insisted on real glasses nothing plastic so Josh had had to hire those. Josh and Frank would keep the profit from the drink sales but pay one third of those profits to the Royal Sisters towards the cost of the ball. On the left would be a line of waiters and waitresses dressed the same as the bar staff. With the girls in black cocktail dresses with a string of pearls and pearl clip on earrings leant to them by Karl and Kris. In front of the bar area were the rows of tables either side of a walking aisle to the dance floor. When they looked up, they would think they were gazing up to the sky above, because the vaulted ceiling was jet black covered in little tiny lights that looked like sparkling stars. The whole marquee was beautifully lit all the way around it was stunning. A professional stage lighting team had been hired, a small 6 piece local orchestra which specialised in music from the 1940's with John Bishon as musical director and pianist and an old friend of theirs Billy Webber on the drums making eight musicians. The Stage had also been hired and was a decent height and the catering company had added black sweeping velvet curtains at their side to dress it.

The band call (dress rehearsal) had gone pretty well at 1pm. Karl was extremely strict about the running order and the sound was checked several times. He warned one or two acts that they had to stick to their time slot and not to overrun and spoil the show. He looked at one particular old friend as he said this.

The waiters had put reserved signs on the first 8 tables in the front rows for the residents of Queens Crescent and their guests. The rest could sit where they liked and would have to share. There were a few portable lean on, drink stations dotted near the front of the marquee for people who preferred to stand. Four portable lavatories had been placed in a discreet location behind the marquee.

So, at 4pm Kristabelle and Karl had done a final walk around to check everything was just so, which it was. They had sectioned off a good portion of the summer house with curtains for their own personal changing area, where their costumes and make up and wigs were laid out perfectly ready for tonight's performance. The refrigerated catering vans were due to arrive at 6pm with the canapes for the 200 guests. The selections were extraordinary and elaborate, quite beautiful and had taken the chef from one of Brighton's top restaurants hours to prepare.

Most of this lot will never have seen anything fucking like it dear said Kris to Karl, its looks beautiful doesn't it. Yes, dear it does said Karl, I'm not doing this for other people love I'm doing it for you, for us. 40 odd years we have been in the business think of it as a little tribute to ourselves. Kris got quite choked up and threw his arms around Karl and kissed him. Thank you darling, he said. Now promise me Kris you won't get pissed until after the show. I promise said Kris I'll just have one before we go on for my nerves. Ok and eat something. I don't think I could, not until after the show I'll be sick with nerves said Kris. Come on said Karl, let's go home and have a lay down.

Yo and Roz were showing their final guests to their Yurts, late arrivals from London. Yo had done better than even she or Roz could have imagined that summer. A slow start at the beginning of June soon picked up and word of mouth and good reviews on trip advisor had ensured nearly a full house of 8 women including trans women every week. 90% of the guests had been great, good humoured, had joined in the yoga sessions, took lots of long walks, signed up for poetry reading sessions and art classes at various locations around town. A few had even gone in for the tribal dance workshop at the Dome and were keen to show what they had learned on their return. Yo and the guests sat in a circle clapping while the 4 women danced around a fire pit Roz had built for chilly evenings to show off their new skills.

There had been one or two "madams" as Roz called them. Finger clickers from Islington. The two worse ones were well known Labour MP's, the obese Milly Pricklebury and the one who couldn't add up Lianne Babbette. Yo was in awe of them but Roz wasn't having it. She told them after the 10th demand for extra this or extra that, that they were the same as anybody else, if they didn't like it, they should leave. This is a peace retreat not a Michelin starred restaurant in North London. They were gone the next morning. As shadow cabinet members they had certain perks. Milly Pricklebury had ordered a chauffeur driven car to come and pick them up, after he had stopped off at the off licence for a bottle of single malt whiskey and spring water for her and 8 cans of premade Mojitos for Lianne. He had also been instructed to find a local KFC and buy two family size bucket meals for the journey back to Islington.

6pm

At all the houses in the crescent there was much jollity and laughter going on (well except for Ben and Gordons) They were trying on their costumes having friends around for pre party drinks and they were all getting in the mood for a good time.

Kris and Karl had entered the dressing room before any of the others had arrived. The show didn't start until 9pm but they were going to meet and greet everybody on the door at arrival at 7.30 sharp, so they needed to start getting made up now.

The caterers had now rolled out a full length red

carpet from the entrance to the pavement in Queens Crescent. Down the sides were gold columns roping off the area, so guests had to arrive on the red carpet. Either side of the entrance to the Marquee stood two enormous gold replicas of Oscar.

Kris and Karl looked at themselves in the full length mirror they had carted up from number 7, wow said Kris, you've certainly pulled it out of the bag this time with the wigs and costumes haven't you. We look amazing. Karl had worked for weeks, many hours into the night to recreate the exact dress and wig that Bette Davis wore in the drunk piano scene in 'All about Eve' yards of black taffeta had been structured into the most beautiful party dress as worn by Margot Channing. The hair and makeup exactly the same. Every possible detail had been painstakingly copied even down to the shoes which he had found in a vintage clothes store in the north Lanes area of Brighton. Karl was Margot Channing. He had the voice off pat too.

For Kris he had recreated the beautiful full length red sequined evening gown as worn by Joan Crawford in the 1937 film 'The bride wore red' slimline and tight to the waist, which suited Kris's anorexic figure. Across the shoulders was a red sequined cape attached from shoulder to shoulder by a diamante sash which sparkled like real diamonds, held together by a diamante and deep blue faux sapphire. He had added some padding to the shoulders to give that typical Crawford style but also because Kris was so thin these days, he needed it to wear the dress properly. He looked a million dollars. Karl had decided not to copy the original hairstyle but fitted Kris with a 1940's Joan Crawford hairstyle like Joan had in Mildred Pierce, plus elegant red sequined and diamante buckle evening shoes with a sensible 3 inch heels and a clutch bag to match. Kris had stuck to his promise and only had one drink to steady his nerves.

They made their way from the summer house with gasps and a round of applause from the other entertainers who had started to arrive to get changed and made up. They headed up the staircase and through the back of the marquee and made their way around the back of the stage to the dance floor area. They looked around and walked towards the entrance their eyes taking in every detail. It was perfect. Karl had mastered Bette Davis's sashaying walk to perfection. All the staff were in place and burst into a spontaneous round of applause when they saw the boys walk forwards.

At dead on 7.30pm Karl waved to John Bishon and the orchestra struck up Glenn Millers 'moonlight serenade' Two of the waiters held back the entrance doors and Bette and Joan walked outside to greet the guests. Flashbulbs started popping from the professional photographer's they had hired. They stood either side of a gold statue of Oscar and just smiled at the huge crowd now queuing up behind the roped off entrance to the red carpet. A huge cheer went up and more clapping and cheering. Kris had to bite his lip to stop any tears ruining his makeup. Karl nodded to the door man who unclipped the rope and invited the assembled guests to take a slow stroll down the red carpet and make sure they smiled at the two camera men, plus a few local paparazzi from the evening Argus and G Scene magazine. First down the red carpet were the residents and their guests. Most of them had made an effort, although some considered the golden era more recent and came as more modern film stars.

First down the line was Cecil and Mike as Tarzan and Jane. Not a pretty sight Cecil towered over Mike and had the skinniest legs ever, Mike in just a loin cloth with his tattoos and hairy chest didn't quite cut it either but they didn't care. Kris winced a bit but smiled and shook hands, next were Roz and Yolanda. Roz was dressed in a Calamity Jane costume complete with rifle. Yolanda looked sensational as one of her other heroes, Angelina Jolie minus the trout mouth. She had wanted to do Oprah but refused to black up. Roz convinced her that colour blind casting wouldn't work in this instance. John and Grant came as Bob Hoskins from 'Who framed Roger rabbit' John in a 1940s demob suit and fedora while Grant was Flash Gordon showing his impeccable physique off to full advantage. Kris didn't want to let go of his hand. Ben came in prison fatigues dressed as Morgan Freeman complete with cap to cover his shaved head in the Shawshank redemption, while Gordon was Madonna in full bondage gear with a little leather mini skirt instead of chaps. Behind was Larry dressed as Rhett Butler from 'Gone with the wind' with a false moustache he looked more than a little like Clarke Gable and was very dashing. Alistair came dressed as a Caballero with a black sombrero hat while Renaldo had full matador drag on representing 'The man from la Mancha' From the pub came Harry Harrington dressed as Doris Day in a 1950's white dirndl skirt, sneakers with bobby Sox a blonde wig tied in bunches and sporting a tight T shirt with enormous breasts which had emblazoned on it HAS ANYONE SEEN MY ROCK? Tina struggling bravely behind him was Carmen Miranda with a huge display of fruit on his head and gypsy earrings. They both got a good laugh from the others.

And so, it went on, there was more than a few Dorothy's from the wizard of oz. A few Mae Wests. Several Kirk Douglas's as Spartan, several of them from the more fit of the gay community. The muscle Mary brigade from Davina Lloyds gym. There were three Marylin's A few more Bette's. Even a Bette Midler complete with wheelchair and mermaid costume. It was a colourful crowd. When the guests moved into the marquee there were gasps of delight and admiration, at the beauty of the room. Staff were on hand to offer a glass of Prosecco on arrival. When all two hundred guests were in and had drinks the 10 waiters started circulating with the delicious canapes. The atmosphere was great. The orchestra were playing continually songs from famous films. There was lots of laughter and bonhomie. Kris and Karl were the stars of the night and they both had big crowds around them fighting for their attention. They were both in their element. Guests started sitting at tables and people took to the dance floor. When the orchestra struck up a Tango. Harry looked at Tina and they were off. Showing their skills just like they had at GG's in Benidorm. Only this time after a successful manoeuvre up and down the dance floor, when Harry (Doris) dipped Tina (Carmen) it was a bit violent and dozens of plastic apples and pears started rolling across the dance floor which brought much hilarity from the crowd. Tina was running around like a demented fairy trying to capture the free rolling fruit.

Unfortunately, outside the weather had changed and they're was a storm brewing. The wind from the coast was getting up. Josh and Olly with some of the caterers ran around the outside of the marquee to make sure that everything was well nailed down and secure. It was. Inside nobody had a clue that it had gone from a sunny summers evening to a wet and windy one very quickly, in England you got used to it. It was now 9pm and the show was about to start. Everyone made their way to their seats, with a few preferring to hang around the bar area and chat. Daisy Froglette looking resplendent in a full length navy blue sequined evening dress, made his way across the stage to take to his throne borrowed from the Fawcett Inn. Karl had asked him if he would MC the show. He said he would be delighted.

First up was an old friend of the Royal Sisters from London. A popular act from years ago called Candy Thyme. He had decided to open with a song and then did a tribute act telling jokes in the style of the great drag acts of all time Mrs Shufflewick, Phil Starr and Dockyard Doris. He brought the house down and was a good warm up for the next act a singer the boys had worked with on several tours called Jane McClaverty. A Scottish girl with a voice like Shirley Bassey. Next up for light relief was Toto and Dorothy, the dog act and then, the Royal Sisters in a quick change and a big make up rework came on as Blanche and Jane Hudson The sisters from "Whatever happened to baby Jane", Miming to a tape recording. Blanche (Bette) pushes Jane around the stage in a wheelchair being vile and feeding her the canary and the rat. It was high camp, nostalgic and just as funny as when David Dale and Lily Savage had made the skit famous in London years ago at the Vauxhall tavern and the Black Cap pub in Camden Town. They got huge applause. Then came Lauren Anderson who had them all on the verge of tears singing her Adele tributes, This time though with an orchestra and pianist accompaniment. She blew the roof off. Then a drum roll, and to close the first half said Daisy The boys you have all been waiting for, the winners of Brighton's got talent please give a huge welcome to The Bandit Boyz. A huge cheer went up as the boys looking sexier than ever in their tight jeans and white shirts came bounding on stage to open with "So many men so little time" The dance floor was filled immediately, and everyone was dancing and singing along. They did three numbers closing with 'Don't let the sun go down on me' which again got a standing ovations and bravos. They hugged each other and Josh behind the bar looked down the long room with pride and a lump in his throat.

Back at the pub Frank said to Mary, look its really quiet most of the regulars are up at the party, why don't you and Dolly go upstairs and get changed, I'll carry on here, I'll close at 11 tonight and come up later. Tell Josh will you. Are you sure lurve said Mary, of course I am, go on get yourself dolled up and go and have a good time? Thanks Frank. Come on Dolly come up with me, we are going to the party. When they came down the few customers in the bar gave them wolf whistles. They were not in fancy dress exactly. Dolly was wearing an original 1940's white silk full evening dress with a train she had hooked around her finger and most of her best diamonds. Her hair scrapped back into an elegant

Chignon. She had on a dainty pair of Jimmy Choo white evening sandals encrusted with diamante heels. Mary also looked lovely she had quickly re blow dried her hair, touched up her makeup and wore a full length leopard skin dress which fitted quite tightly on her still fit body. It had thin shoulder straps, which showed off her spray tan beautifully. She had a gold coloured pashmina wrapped around her and leopard skin mules. Lots of chunky gold jewellery and her best glasses which were part of her trademark with enormous white frames.

Frank said ladies you shall go to the ball I'll call you a cab. He handed them two umbrellas from under the bar. Here you had better take these it's a getting a bit wild out there. Oh, gawd is it said Mary I 'ope it doesn't fooking rain, not tonight. Well best be on the safe side said Frank. Have a quick drink before you go. When they arrived, they couldn't believe the effort that had gone into the party. It's beautiful said Dolly. Fooking gorgeous said Mary, I've never seen owt like it in me life. They took a glass of prosecco each from a waiter, just then Mary spotted the buffet table where the waiters had laid out the remaining canapes for the guests to nibble on. Steering Dolly in the direction of the food. Mary spotted a tray of prawn vol au vents, quick as a flash she had grabbed four of them with a napkin and shoved them into her handbag. Dolly didn't even notice. There were some little silver cruet sets there too, so she had one of them, they'd look nice on her breakfast tray in the morning. Fancy a dance ladies said Harry Harrington? walking towards them with Tina tits. Not dressed like that you cont, said Mary. Thank you, boys I'll pass too, said Dolly. Suit yerselves then said Harry haughtily, he was a bit drunk now and spotted a Rock

Hudson lookalike near the bar and was off like a shot. Sidling up to 'Rock' he pointed at his breasts with the "Has anyone seen my Rock" slogan on, Rock took one look at 'Doris Day' and turned his back on Harry. You never did that in pillow talk did you said Harry? Come on said Tina let's get another drink.

The second half was about to start. The whole set was just 'The Royal Sisters'. They did 45 minutes of all their best loved songs from the past 40 years. Their impersonations of Mae West, Marlene, Judy Garland and Dorothy Squires brought the house down. They didn't finish with 'What makes a man a man' because they wanted to change back into their Bette and Joan outfits for the rest of the party and didn't want to re do the make up again. Three times in one night was enough. So, they closed with 'The best of times' from the musical 'La cage aux folles' and the whole crowd joined in for a sing song. Some had tears streaming down their faces as the whole atmosphere was charged with emotion and of course alcohol. They took 8 curtain calls, before the orchestra struck up with some famous dance tunes from the golden era. Couples took to the floor and danced until two o'clock in the morning. It was the party to end all parties. Kris and Karl hugged each other tightly in their sectioned off bit of the summerhouse and both wept tears of joy. It's been perfect said Kris. Thank you for being my partner for forty years said Karl. No thank you said Kris I don't know what I'd do without you, I really don't. We need to take a year off now said Karl, get your weight sorted out, get you dried out and go somewhere on holiday that's quiet, just on our own. We need a rest. I won't argue with that said Kris, but tonight I'm going to party like I have never done before. Are you ready for our entrance? As they headed for the back of the Marquee there was a strike of lightening a loud clap of thunder and the heavens opened. Quick said Karl they just made it inside in time.

Yo, and Roz had left the party at about 11.30pm, they had to see to their guests in the morning and were tired. Come on Roz lets go back, it's been great but its nearly all gay men here, we've shown our faces lets go home. Roz downed her pint of Kronenburg said come on then. They snuck out and would say their thank you's tomorrow. Walking back to number 2, Yo said do you mind if I sleep in my yurt tonight Roz, it's very humid and sticky it would be nice to be outside. Oh, love do you have to said Roz she was hoping for a little leg over before sleep. Yes, I just want to meditate and unwind. I don't think I could sleep inside tonight with this humidity. Oh, alright said Roz, if that's what you want, Yo, leant over and kissed her. Thanks babe said Yo. Yo didn't meditate for long she was fast asleep in 10 minutes dead to the world. Roz though had poured a glass of scotch and taken it up to bed. She was laying on top of the bed just pondering when she saw a flash of lightening, followed quickly by a massive clap of thunder. Jesus, she thought, and then the rain came, she got up and went to the window pulling the curtains right back she loved a good storm but this one was a bit close. The wind had got up too. She looked down to the garden to check on the yurts. They were waving a bit in the gale. I wonder if they will all be alright down there, she worried. Just then another clap of thunder and a huge gust of wind got under one of the yurts and lifted it right out of the ground and blew it towards the rear of the garden clipping Yo's yurt and ending up in the strip of field behind the houses. Yo woke up with a start, oh dear god what's happening she muttered, she reached for her jeans and started to pull them on. Roz looked down in horror at the scene below her bedroom window. The disappearing yurt had exposed its inhabitants in all of their glory. She was witnessing an orgy. She shone a torch out of the window and saw a pair of hairy buttocks pumping away for all it was worth. What the fuck said Roz out loud. Sharon, the woman who hadn't transformed yet and was still in the early stages of gender realignment was fucking the arse off of Caz, doggie style, Caz a bisexual woman, had her head buried between the legs of Maureen who was born a man but now a woman who had had the full gender realignment done several years ago. Roz ran down the stairs as fast as she could, she opened the back door and grabbed the fire bucket full of water. Yo came stumbling up the garden and witnessed the same scene Roz had from the bedroom, she watched in horror as Roz chucked the fire bucket full of water over the three of them, who were so stoned they hadn't even noticed the storm. However, the ice cold water from the bucket made them come to. Sharon said what the fuck do you think you are doing? I think that's the question I'd like to ask you said Roz how dare you do that here. Caz pulled a hair from her mouth and said oh chill out you old dyke. With that Roz waded in and punched Caz straight in the mouth. Maureen meanwhile was trying to retain some dignity by pulling a yoga mat over her lady garden. Yo horrified and dripping wet said. I think you had all better come into the kitchen right now. Caz was crying, you hit me! you hit me you bitch I'll have you arrested. Want another one you fucking whore said Roz. Please Roz please stop it, stop it right now.

Everyone grab something to wear and come inside said Yo. Roz still with her temper up said this is supposed to be a peaceful retreat for women not a fucking brothel. Peaceful said Maureen with all that racket going on over there pointing in the direction of the marquee. Shh now everyone please come inside said Yo. The rain had stopped but they were all dripping wet. Yo ran up to the airing cupboard to grab some towels, she told Roz to go into the sitting room and calm down. The other bedraggled three came in through the back door and Yo handed out the towels. She went to the freezer and got some ice and wrapped it in a tea towel and handed it to Caz. Here now sit down all of you and let me think. Yo had gone straight into full teacher mode in a crisis. Roz yelled from the sitting room I want them all out of here NOW! Yo went into her and said shut up Roz you've done enough damage let me sort this out. She went back into the kitchen and said well who's going to explain this awful scene we had to witness? It turned out that the three of them had been doing drugs, Sharon had rolled a thick joint with some black leb hash she had scored outside the town hall earlier where there was a hippy market selling crafts and vegan food. Maureen had bought a bottle of brandy in case it got cold in the yurt and Caz had a little bag of cocaine with her. They had put on some Joan Armatrading music and got stoned. One thing had led to another. Caz mentioned she still liked a bit of cock now and again and Sharon offered to oblige. Maureen said what about me? So, Caz offered to sort Maureen out and Sharon had promised to slip Maureen a portion after Caz. But that's disgusting said Yo. Why said Sharon? Well this is a peace retreat for meditation and healing not a knocking shop. Well we are all consenting adults said Caz, and you! said Yo pointing at Sharon, you have not had the op yet, you are still a man. Oh no I'm not said Sharon indignantly, I identify as a woman I always have, and when I have my operation, I shall become what I know I have always been, a lesbian. For once Yo was lost for words. If Sharon identified as a woman/ lesbian even though she still had a large cock and a hairy bottom that was her right. Yo was a little confused, she wondered if the BBC had a support page about this on their website. Nothing she had learned on her diversity courses had prepared her for this situation.

Right I'm going to make us all a cup of tea. Yo put the kettle on and decided what she was going to do. She handed around the cups of tea. Ok, well I have to respect your decisions to identify as who you want to be. Your use of pronouns and your decision to be non-binary is your choice alone. However, I am incredibly angry about the use of drugs on my premises. Luckily for you the other tenants in the next yurt are still out god knows where at the moment and didn't hear your cavorting's. Sharon, Caz and Maureen all looked subdued and worn out. Here is what we are going to do. Sharon you can have my Yurt, it is still standing and didn't get wet inside. You two can share the guest bedroom which has twin beds, but no more sexual activity for tonight ok? Sure, said Caz still holding the T Towel to her mouth. Promise said Yo? Cross me heart said Sharon forgetting his falsetto voice and sounding now like a tired Lorry driver. I promise simpered Maureen very contrite. What about your Mrs said Caz, she shouldn't have thumped me? No, my partner, shouldn't have and I apologise for that, but you did insult her. However, Caz you are fucking lucky I'm offering you a bed for the night and haven't reported you to the police for cocaine possession and taking other illegal substances. Ok said Caz fair enough I'm knackered where's the bedroom. I'll show you up now said Yo. Come on Maureen you too. Sharon there's a torch on the sink you can see yourself out. Ok said Sharon. Breakfast will be in here in the kitchen at 8.30pm, then I want you all off of the premises. Is that clear? They all nodded.

Yo went into Roz who had fallen asleep on the Sofa. Yo gently woke her, Roz stirred and then remembered, what a fucking night off that was for me thanks Yo she said. I'm sorry said Yo. She explained the situation and about Sharon identifying as a lesbian even though she still had the full tackle. Roz started to laugh; she couldn't stop, tears running down her face. Yo cracked a smile but was uneasy. Honestly Yo, you don't half believe some bullshit. Do you know it would do you good to get away from all your woke friends for a few months and get out in the real world and see what's really going on. You're so wrapped up in your metropolitan world of Guardian readers, BBC friends, Brighton and north London politics that you can't see what's going on outside that bubble. Yo looked like she had been struck. I'm sorry Yo I love you but sometimes this politically correct shit gets right on my tits. Where are they now? When Yo told her that Caz and Maureen were upstairs. Roz thought she would explode again. Instead she took a deep breath and said, I want those Yurts gone as soon as possible, I'm going to bed, and I shall stay there until all your weirdo fucking guests have gone. She slammed the door on her way out. Yo was upset, Roz had never spoken to her like that before, she curled up into a little ball pulled the sofa throw on top of her and cried herself to sleep.

Back at the marquee things were starting to come to a close. It was now 1.45 am and people had started drifting off about 1.30 am. There was a long wait for taxis. Everybody had complimented Kristabelle and Karl for the party. All agreed it was the best party they had ever been to. The Royal Sisters could not have asked for more. They went around and thanked all the staff personally. They stood at the door until the last guests left at 2.20am. They went over to the bar cracked open a bottle of champagne and kicked their shoes off. Tomorrow they would plan their future.

September 3rd

Alister and Renaldo were packing up their last box. The removal van was due any minute to take all of their things over to Spain. They had sold and were due to complete later today. Monday the 3rd of September. Nobody was expecting any hold ups, the buyer was a cash buyer with no chain. The house had sold within a month of going up for sale. They had two open days and three offers. The one they accepted was a cash buyer who was not in a chain, so no mortgage to arrange either. They had flown out to Spain the week after Pride in August and rented a lovely villa on the outskirts of Valencia city, it had a pool and a nice garden. They had the opportunity to buy it if they liked it after 6 months. Renaldo had applied and got a job to teach English and Spanish at the international school. They had arranged for Sky tv to be installed using their Sky pass from England. Alistair could still watch talking pictures in the afternoon. They had kept very quiet about who they had sold to and told nobody, not even Mike and Cecil. In fact, they had never met them as they had gone out at the time of the viewings and let the estate agents handle all the negotiations. As the removal van pulled away at about four o'clock, they locked the door for the last time, both had a lump in their throats. They handed over the keys to the estate agent then popped around to say goodbye to Cecil and Mike. Some of the others had wished them good luck from their doorsteps and waved. They had a stiff drink with Mike and Cecil and said we will see you in Spain. They said, we hope you get on with the new neighbours, who is it said Cecil? Well all I know really is that it's a professional couple said Alistair. A gay couple I hope said Mike. I really have no idea about that said Alistair. They called a taxi to take them up to Gatwick, they were going to spend the night at the airport then fly to Valencia the next morning, have two days in a hotel there and be at the villa Thursday afternoon to meet the removal company at the other end. They all hugged each other goodbye. Renaldo got a bit emotional and that started Cecil off. They waved their friends goodbye as they set off to find their place in the sun.

Epilogue.

Ben had decided to work from home on Monday and

Gordon got back from Mission Accomplished at 5.30 pm. Ben was out in the front garden pruning back some bushes and plants ready for the winter. At 6 o'clock three large removal lorries pulled up outside of number 6. Ben looked up and banged on the window to Gordon and beckoned him to come outside. Gordon joined him and said three lorries that's a lot of stuff. I do hope it is someone nice. Just then a vivid pink huge SUV swept into the drive. A woman in her 40's got out followed by a very fit young man in his 20's and three children clutching McDonalds meal deal bags who started running around and shouting. The woman turned around to the children and said shut the fuck up you lot. Let me get the fucking door open before you start. Gordon looked at Ben in horror. Do you know who that is he said? I know the face said Ben. That's Katrina Rice, the page three model, dear god please don't let it be her she's as common as muck said Gordon.

It was Katrina Rice the millionaire model. She had been through some bad times lately had two expensive divorces, her career had taken a nosedive, so she sold her stately home in the Cotswolds and moved to Brighton to be near her mum.

She saw the boys looking over at her and came over to say hello. Hello, I'm Katrina she said walking around to the front of number 5. I'm your new neighbour, that's my new fiancé Shane, wave Shaney she yelled at the top of her voice. Shane gave them a cursory nod. Who are you? Ben introduced themselves. Fuck me you're a hottie you are aren't you she said to Ben. Once you've had black there's no looking back eh mate? she said to Gordon winking with a dirty smile. Gordon couldn't answer he was in shock. He was staring at Katrina's drooping trout pout mouth and over enlarged breasts that looked like two giant footballs. She was only about 5 foot 1 and they looked hideous. Oh well I had better go, the kids will be smashing something up by now and I had better let the removal men get in. Come on lads shift yer bleedin' arses she yelled to the removal men. They all laughed they had moved her several times before she was a good laugh and some of them had fantasised about her in their teens. You'll 'ave to come 'rand' for our housewarming she said to Ben and Gordon. I'll get the hot tub set up and then all me family and loads of me mates are coming round for a dip and a karaoke session, you'll love it. This place looks like it needs livening up. See ya she said walking away. She winked at them pushed her breasts together, licked her lips seductively and blew them a kiss.

Gordon felt sick he ran inside the house and poured himself and Ben a large brandy. Oh god I really don't believe it, Katrina Rice it couldn't be any worse. Bad enough they are heterosexual with bloody kids, but her dear god she's about as common as you can get. The prices will drop around here having hetero's living in the street. Those kids look like hooligans we won't be safe to go out said Gordon working himself up into a right state. He started pacing the floor. Before you know it there will be Asda delivery vans arriving (Gordon only used Ocado) and Pizza deliveries night and day. What the hell are we going to do. Ben also a bit shocked was noticeably quiet his mind was going into overdrive at what to do next.

They were not the only ones to feel distressed. With the exception of John and Grant who already had kids and Olly and Will, the same sort of reaction was being felt along the Crescent. Much speculation on having straight people living in Queens Crescent, what it would do to property prices, How Katrina Rice would lower the tone, the bother of paparazzi. Many of them not realising they were stating the same sort of ignorant prejudices that people had said about them in a different era.

Ben and Gordons relationship didn't survive. Ben couldn't cope with Gordons snobbism anymore. He moved up to London, rented a service flat in Vauxhall near to an S&M leather club where he could live out his fantasies. He contacted the police anonymously and gave them information which led to the arrest of Florim, his girlfriend Bora, Durak and eight other Albanian drug dealers. They were going to be deported after a lengthy prison sentence. However, one of Bens colleagues was already working on getting that overturned. He left the company he worked for, then opened up an office near the Asylum seekers support centre in Croydon. He set up on his own making mega bucks from legal aid overturning home office deportation orders. He still dated Simon occasionally. Gordon couldn't get a big enough mortgage to cover the repayments on his own, plus he couldn't bear living next door to "that old whore" anyway. So, the house went up for sale. He was busy looking for a stylish flat to suit his status and where he could relocate the dungeon to. Larry had become keen on S&M too and had taken Bens place as master.

Kristabelle checked into the Priory for a month to be dried out and have psychiatric help to try and cure his bulimia. Once he was stable, they took off for three weeks to the Seychelles and just rested. They then rented a luxury villa in Mallorca near Port Soler for 6 months. They had stashed plenty of money away over the years, they were always paid in cash so they could afford to take a break. They were planning a big farewell tour before retirement.

Yolanda had made quite a bit of money from her Yurt BnB experiment. Roz said it was over and she meant it. However, Yo had enjoyed the business and took Roz on a kayaking holiday to Vietnam to sweeten her up.

Frank and Josh carried on as normal although Josh was often away on tour with the Bandit Boyz, who were now enjoying a taste of success, they were busy promoting a new single and were doing lots of TV interviews. They were on the up. Harry had met an older man in his late 30's while they were on tour and fell in love. When he told Frank and Josh, they both gave him their blessing.

When the story broke about the MP Paul Bryan. The media went crazy. It was the number one story on all of the news stations and the front page of every newspaper. Paul Bryan didn't give a fuck. He revelled in the notoriety. His job was safe as Jeremy Corbyn refused to sack him saying that what he did in his private life was up to him. However, his constituents would soon be showing him the door with a vote of no confidence. John and Grant decided to disappear for a bit and took the kids to Disney world in Florida for three weeks.

Cecil and Michael still went to Bingo every Friday. They were looking forward to staying a week with Alistair and Renaldo in Valencia before a week in Beni with the Duchess in the spring next year.

Ollie and Will carried on the same, they were happy in love and content. They didn't care like the others about Katrina Rice moving into the street, live and let live was their motto. They always enjoyed a happy ending.

Katrina and Shane didn't stay for long. After 9 months a for sale sign went up again. She knew where she wasn't wanted. She had been frozen out by most of the neighbours, there were no other children to play with her three. So, she moved yet again to a smartish part of Hove where her neighbours were Chris Ewbank and where some of the cast of EastEnders lived, she fitted in well with them. Shaney got dumped and another one just the same was moved in.

The Fawcett Inn stayed busy. Daisy Froglette carried on with the Sunday school and she and Alanna Cardinal were sifting through the talent and planning next year's Brighton's got Talent. Tina tits and Harry Harrington were at a front table every week getting sloshed and camping it up after they had cleaned all the rooms at the hotel. Harry was sporting a black eye recently as a customer had caught him looking thorough a gap in the door as the man got undressed. Harry had been pretending to be down on all fours with a dustpan and brush looked up just as the man slammed the door shut. The doorknob hit Harry straight in the right eye.

Mary and Dolly had already been out to Spain to see Gemma, who was incredibly happy playing housewife and milking goats. As Mary said to Josh on their return. 'es as 'appy as a pig in shit darlin' She carried on working as usual, she still had her Monday club where her clients kept coming back for more, including pissy Michael and 'Herman the German' Ralph who had come for a month and never gone back. Mary and Dolly were busy planning their next adventure. Instead of Benidorm they were going to do a road trip through America, the famous Route 66. We'll be just like Thelma and Louise said Mary it'll be fooking marvellous lurve.

The End

Also, by the same Author on Amazon are

The boy from Primrose hill
(autobiography)

Printed in Poland
by Amazon Fulfillment
Poland Sp. z o.o., Wrocław

62496457R00117